THE BLIND-DATE
PROPOSAL

THE BLIND-DATE PROPOSAL

BY

JESSICA HART

MILLS & BOON®

*MILLS & BOON and
MILLS & BOON with the Rose Device
are registered trademarks of the publisher.*

*First published in Great Britain 2003
Large Print edition 2003
Harlequin Mills & Boon Limited,
Eton House, 18-24 Paradise Road,
Richmond, Surrey TW9 1SR*

© Jessica Hart 2003

ISBN 0 263 17953 2

*Set in Times Roman 16½ on 17 pt.
16-1103-53630*

*Printed and bound in Great Britain
by Antony Rowe Ltd, Chippenham, Wiltshire*

CHAPTER ONE

'WHAT time do you call this?'

Finn looked up, scowling, as Kate knocked on his door with some trepidation.

She looked at her watch. 'It's…er…nearly quarter to ten.'

'And you're supposed to start at what time?'

'Nine o'clock.'

Kate was horribly aware of her pink face. She was hot and flustered, having run up the escalator from the tube and all the way to the office, where she had panted past the surprised receptionist to fall into the lift. Somewhere along the line she had laddered her tights, and a tentative glance in the mirror was enough to confirm that her hair, a mass of wild brown curls hard to control at best of times, was tangled and windblown.

Not a good start to the day.

She was at a distinct disadvantage compared to Finn, too. In his grey suit and his pristine shirt, her new boss had always seemed to Kate buttoned up in more ways than one. He had a severe face, steely grey eyes and strong dark brows which were usually pulled together in a frown and whenever he looked at Kate, like now, his mouth was clamped together in a disapproving line.

'I know I'm late, and I'm *really* sorry,' she said breathlessly and, oblivious to Finn's discouraging expression, she launched into a long and convoluted explanation of how she had befriended an elderly lady confused by the underground system and intimidated by the rudeness of officials.

'I couldn't just leave her there,' she finished at last, 'so I took her to Paddington and showed her where to find her train.'

'Paddington not being on your way here?'

'Not *exactly*…'

'One might even say that it was in completely the opposite direction,' Finn went on in the same snide tone.

'Not quite *opposite*,' said Kate, mentally consulting her tube map.

'So you got halfway here and then turned and headed off in a completely different direction, even though you must have known that there was no way you'd be able to get to work on time?'

'I had to,' Kate protested. 'She was so upset. There was no reason for everyone to be so rude to her,' she remembered indignantly. 'Her English wasn't that good, and she couldn't be expected to know where she was going and how to get there. How would that ticket collector like it if he had to find his way around...oh, I don't know...the Amazon, say...where he didn't know the language and nobody could be bothered to help him?'

Finn looked at her wearily. 'You're mistaking me for someone who cares,' he said. 'The only thing I care about right now is keeping this company going, and it's not that easy with a PA who turns up whenever she feels like it! Alison makes a point of arriving ten minutes before nine every day,' he added pointedly. 'She's always reliable.'

Not so reliable that she didn't break her leg on a skiing holiday, Kate thought, but didn't say out loud. She was sick of hearing about Alison, Finn's perfect PA who was discreet and efficient and immaculately dressed and who reputedly typed at the speed of light. She could probably read Finn's mind too, Kate had decided sourly after he had shouted at her for not being able to find a file that he himself had dumped onto her desk. Alison's desk, of course, was always tidy.

The only marvel was that Alison had been careless enough to break her leg, leaving Finn to get through eight weeks without her.

He wasn't finding it easy. Already two temps had left in tears, unable to cope with the impossible standards Alison had set. Kate was just surprised that she had hung in as long as she had. This was her third week and, judging by Finn's expression, it might well be her last.

She wasn't surprised the others had given up. Finn McBride gave a whole new dimension to the notion of grumpiness and he had an unpleasantly sarcastic edge to his tongue. If she hadn't been desperate for a job, she would have been tempted to walk out on him as well.

'I said I was sorry,' she said a little sullenly. 'Not that I should have to apologise for community spirit,' she went on, still too fired up by her encounter that morning to be able to summon up the correct degree of subservience that no doubt came naturally to Alison.

Finn was unimpressed. His cold grey eyes raked her from head to foot, taking in every detail of her tangled hair and dishevelled clothes and stopping with exasperation on her laddered tights.

'I encourage my staff to do what I pay them to do,' he said frigidly, 'and that's what they do. You, on the other hand, appear to think that I should pay you to breeze in and distract everyone else in the office all day.'

Kate gaped at the unfairness of it. She had made efforts to get to know the rest of the staff, but without any great success. They didn't seem to be great ones for gossiping and, on the few occasions she had managed to strike up a conversation, Finn had been safely shut in his office. He must have X-ray eyes if he had noticed her talking to anyone!

'I don't distract anyone,' she protested.

'It sounds that way to me,' said Finn. 'You're always out in the corridor or in the other offices chatting.'

'It's called social interaction,' said Kate, provoked. 'It's what humans do, not that you'd know that of course. It's like working with robots in this office,' she went on, forgetting for a moment how much she needed this job. 'I'm lucky if I get a good morning from you, and even that I have to translate from a grunt!'

The dark brows twitched together into a terrifying glare. 'Alison never complains.'

'Maybe Alison likes being treated like just another piece of office equipment,' she said tartly. 'It wouldn't kill you to show a little interest occasionally.'

Finn glowered at her, and Kate wondered whether he was so unused to anyone daring to argue with him that he was taken aback.

If so, he soon recovered. 'I haven't time to waste the day bolstering your ego,' he snapped.

'It doesn't take long to be pleasant.' Kate refused to be cowed now. 'You could always start with something easy like "how are you?", or "have a nice weekend",' she suggested. 'And then, when you'd got the hang of that, you could work up to trickier phrases like "thank you for all your help today".'

'I can't see me having much need of that one while you're around,' said Finn nastily. 'And frankly, even if I did, I don't see why I should change my habits for you. In case you haven't noticed, I'm the boss here, so if you can't cope without constant attention, you'd better say so now and I'll get Personnel to find me another temp for Monday!'

That was enough to pull Kate up short. She really couldn't afford to lose this job. The agency had been reluctant enough to send her as it was and, if she messed this up, she'd be lucky if they didn't drop her from their books.

'I can cope,' she said quickly. 'I just don't like it.'

'You don't have to like it,' said Finn tersely. 'You just have to get on with it. Now, can we get on? We've wasted quite enough time this morning.'

He barely allowed Kate time to take off her coat before she had to endure a long and exhausting session being dictated to at top speed without so much as a suggestion that she might like a cup of coffee before she started. What with befriending old ladies and diversions to Paddington, she hadn't had time to grab her usual cappuccino from the Italian coffee bar by the tube station, and the craving for caffeine did nothing to improve her temper.

She simmered as her pen raced over the page—at this rate she would get repetitive strain injury—and could barely restrain a sigh of relief when the phone rang. A breather at last!

Holding her aching wrist with exaggerated care, so that Finn might take the hint and slow down—although there was fat chance of that!—Kate studied him surreptitiously under her lashes. He was listening to the person on the other end of the phone, grunting the occasional acknowledgement, and absently drawing heavy black boxes on a piece of paper on the desk in front of him.

Doodling was supposed to be highly revealing about your personality. What did black boxes mean? Kate wondered. Probably indicative of someone deeply repressed. That would fit with his closed expression and that reserved uptight air of his.

Although not with that air of fierce energy. Or his mouth, come to think of it.

Kate jerked her eyes quickly away. She looked instead at the framed photograph that stood on his desk, the only personal touch in the otherwise austerely efficient office. From where she sat, she could only see the stand, but she knew it showed an absolutely beautiful woman with dark hair and enormous dark blue eyes, holding the most gorgeous baby, and both smiling at the camera.

Finn's wife, Kate had assumed, marvelling that he had had enough social skills to ask anyone to marry him, let alone a beauty like that. It was hard to imagine him smiling or kissing or even holding a baby, let alone making love.

Bizarre thought. An odd feeling snaked down Kate's spine and she shook herself slightly, only to find herself looking straight into Finn's glacial grey eyes. He had finished his phone call while she was distracted and was watching her with an expression of exasperated resignation.

'Are you awake?'

'Yes.' Faint colour tinged Kate's cheeks as she sat up straighter and picked up her notebook once more.

'Read back that last bit.'

Please, Kate wanted to mutter, but decided on reflection that this might not be the day to try and teach Finn some manners. His brusqueness left her feeling crotchety and, when he finally let her go, she took out her bad temper on her keyboard, bashing away furiously until the phone rang.

'Yes?' she snapped, too cross to bother with the usual introductory spiel.

'It's Phoebe.'

'Oh, Phoebe…hi.'

'What's up? You sound very grumpy.'

'It's just my boss here,' Kate grumbled. 'He's so rude and unpleasant. I know you thought working for Celia was bad, but honestly, he gives a whole new dimension to the idea of the boss from hell.'

'As long as he's not a creep like your last boss,' said Phoebe bracingly.

Kate wrinkled her nose remembering her ignominious departure from her last job, where

her boss hadn't even made a pretence of listening to her side of the story once Seb had
got in first. Seb, of course, was an executive,
and she was just a secretary and by implication
dispensable.

'No, I don't think you could call him a
creep,' she said judiciously, 'but that doesn't
make him any easier to deal with.'

'Attractive?' asked Phoebe.

'Quite,' Kate admitted grudgingly. 'In a
stern sort of way, I suppose. If you like the
dour, my-work-is-my-life type—which I happen to know that you don't!'

'I don't think anyone could call Gib dour,
no,' said Phoebe.

They both laughed, and Kate felt a lot better.
It was wonderful to hear Phoebe so happy. The
transformation in her friend since she had married Gib a few months ago had been remark-
able, and it made up for her own dismal love
life since Seb had dumped her so unceremo-
niously. She didn't even get wolf-whistles in
the street any more, Kate thought glumly.

'I was just ringing to remind you about supper tonight,' Phoebe was saying. 'You are
coming, aren't you?'

'Of course,' said Kate, but Phoebe pounced
on her momentary hesitation.

'What?'

'Well, it's just that Bella hinted that you might be setting me up on a blind date to-night.'

'She shouldn't have told you!' Phoebe sounded really cross. 'I only told her because I invited her and Josh as well so it would seem more casual, but she's met some new man who's taking her to some swanky club tonight instead. Josh is coming, though,' she added re-assuringly, 'so it won't be too much of a set-up.'

'Why didn't you tell me?'

'Because I wanted you both to be natural, and I knew you wouldn't be if you were ner-vous about whether he liked you or not.'

'Hhmmnn.' Kate wasn't entirely convinced. 'What have you told him about me?'

'That you're a high-powered PA—which you could easily be if you put your mind to it!' said Phoebe. 'He's got his own consultancy or something, so I wasn't sure if he'd be that impressed by you temping, but apart from that we told him the truth, the whole truth and nothing but the truth,' she finished virtuously.

'Oh, the *truth*!' said Kate, her voice heavy with irony. 'And what's that, exactly?'

'That you're warm and funny and attractive and basically completely wonderful,' Phoebe said firmly.

Perhaps she should ask Phoebe to put in some PR for her with Finn McBride, Kate thought, and then frowned slightly as she realised that she had been unconsciously doodling in her turn as she listened to Phoebe.

At least she didn't go in for severe black boxes. She had done her favourite, a tropical sunset complete with leaning palm tree and a couple of wiggly lines to indicate the lagoon rippling gently against the shore. What did that indicate about her?

Probably that she was a hopeless fantasist, in which case she could save herself the cost of a professional analysis. She already knew that she was far too romantic for her own good. People had been telling her for years that she needed to shape up, get real, wake up and smell the coffee, and do all the other things that simply didn't come naturally to her.

Suppressing a sigh, Kate carefully added a bunch of coconuts to the palm tree. 'So won't he wonder why if I'm that perfect I'm reduced to being set up on blind dates by friends? Why aren't men falling at my feet wherever I go?'

'I don't know. Why aren't they?'

That was one of the things Kate liked about Phoebe. She really believed in her friends.

Kate put down her pen and forced herself to concentrate. Perhaps all this was a sign to stop dreaming about Seb miraculously turning into a different person and to start making an effort to meet someone new. To wake up and smell the coffee, in fact.

'So what's he like, this guy?'

'I've never met him,' Phoebe had to admit. 'He's an old friend of Gib's.'

'How old, exactly?'

'In his early forties, I think.'

'Just coming up for his mid-life crisis then,' said Kate with an uncharacteristic touch of cynicism.

'He's already had more than enough crises,' said Phoebe soberly. 'He's a widower. His wife died when their daughter was just a toddler, and he's been struggling to bring her up on his own ever since.'

'Oh, how awful,' said Kate, her ready sympathy roused and feeling instantly guilty for her flip comment. 'It must have been terrible for him.'

'Well, yes, I gather it was. Gib says he absolutely adored his wife, but it's six years ago now, and he's thinking that his little girl is getting to the stage when she really needs a woman around. He's out of the way of dating, though, and since you were complaining about not meeting any men, Gib suggested a casual supper to introduce you. It's no big deal, but he thought you might get on.'

'I don't know that I'm really stepmother material,' said Kate doubtfully. 'I don't know anything about children.'

'Nonsense!' Phoebe wasn't having any of that. 'Look how good you are with animals, and children are just the same. They need someone to take them under her wing, and you know what a soft heart you've got for lame ducks.'

'Yes, but I don't want to go out with a lame duck,' Kate protested. 'I want someone sexy and exciting and glamorous.'

Like Seb.

The same thought was clearly in Phoebe's mind. 'No you don't,' she said firmly. 'You want someone kind.'

Kate sighed. 'Why can't I have someone who's kind *and* sexy and exciting and glamorous?'

'Because I married him,' said Phoebe smugly. 'Now listen, this guy's had a hard time, so be nice to him.'

'Oh, all right,' grumbled Kate. 'What's his name, anyway—' She broke off as Finn's door opened. 'Uh-oh, here comes Mr Grumpy! I'd better go—I'm not supposed to use the phone for personal calls. See you later.' She put the phone down hastily.

Finn looked at her with a suspicious frown. 'Who was that?'

Well, she wasn't going to tell him the truth and, although she could have made up something innocuous, Kate had an irrepressibly inventive streak and as a matter of principle resisted the simple option when she could complicate matters. She embarked instead on a long, involved and utterly untrue story, inventing an accountant who had met Alison skiing but who had subsequently been on a business trip to Singapore and had only just heard about the accident and, remembering that Alison had told him where she worked, now wanted to know where to send a card.

'I said it would be all right if he sent it here and we would forward it,' she finished, having embroidered the story with so many details that she almost believed it herself.

Finn's expression was glazed with irritation by the time she got to the end. 'I wish I'd never asked,' he sighed. 'You've just wasted a quarter of an hour of my life!'

'It's not as if we do brain surgery here,' said Kate, a trifle sullenly. 'I don't see what difference fifteen minutes here or there makes.'

'In that case, you won't mind staying late tonight to make up for the hour you missed this morning,' Finn said with an unpleasant look. 'We've got an extremely important project coming up and I need to get this done to fax to the States before tomorrow morning.'

'I can't, I'm afraid,' she said, not sounding at all regretful. 'I'm going out.'

Finn frowned. 'Can't you ring and say you'll be a bit late?'

For anyone else, Kate would have offered to do just that, but something about Finn McBride rubbed her up the wrong way. It wasn't as if he had made the slightest effort to be pleasant to her.

'Oh, I don't think my boyfriend would like that very much,' she said instead, trying for the unconscious smugness that so often seemed to accompany the words 'my boyfriend'.

'You've got a boyfriend?' Finn was unflatteringly surprised, and Kate bridled. It was bad enough putting up with his rudeness without knowing that he thought her incapable of attracting a man as well!

'Oh, yes,' she said, determined to convince him that while she might not be a perfect PA, *somebody* wanted her. 'In fact,' she went on, leaning forward confidentially, 'he's taking me somewhere really special tonight. I think he might be going to pop the question!'

'Really?' Finn raised a contemptuous eyebrow, not even bothering to try and hide his disbelief.

How rude, thought Kate indignantly. He clearly didn't think she was the kind of girl who would get a man at all, let alone one who wanted to marry her.

Her brown eyes narrowed. 'Oh, yes,' she said on her mettle. 'Didn't you know? That's why I'm temping. Ever since I met—'

She searched wildly for a name before remembering Bella's current and very glamorous man. Your best friend's boyfriend was normally out of bounds, but she didn't think Bella would mind her borrowing him mentally.

'—Will,' she carried on after the tiniest beat, 'we've both known that we were meant for each other. He's a financial analyst,' she went on breezily, deciding that she might as well take Will's career as well, 'so I didn't want to commit to a permanent job when he might be posted to New York or Tokyo at any minute. Of course, he keeps saying to me, ''Darling, there's no need for you to go out to work every day,'' but I feel it's important to keep some financial independence, don't you?'

'I wouldn't have thought your earnings as a temp would make much difference if you're living with a financial analyst,' said Finn with something not a million miles from a sneer.

'It's a matter of principle,' said Kate airily, quite enjoying the thought of herself destined for a life of expatriate luxury.

Finn turned back to his office. 'Perhaps you could make it a matter of principle to turn up on time tomorrow,' he said nastily. 'That would make a nice change.'

It was a pity she wasn't as good at real life as she was at inventing it, Kate reflected glumly as the bus inched through the rush hour traffic, vibrating noisily. Wouldn't it be nice to be going home to a real adoring man with pots of money and to be told that she never had to go and work for the likes of Finn McBride ever again?

Kate sighed and rubbed the condensation from the window with her sleeve and peered down at the crowds hurrying along Piccadilly in the rain. They all seemed to know exactly where they were going. Why was she the only one who drifted along from one muddle to the next?

Look at her. Thirty-two and what did she have to show for it? No career, no home of her own, no relationship. The only thing she had gained over the last few years was twenty pounds. Even the misery diet hadn't worked for her. When their hearts got broken the weight fell off her friends, but comfort eating had been the only way Kate could deal with losing Seb and her job together before Christmas. A double whammy.

Fortified by Bella and Phoebe and a good deal of champagne, Kate had resolved that things would change in the New Year. She was going to sharpen up her act. She would get another, better job and another, better man, she vowed. She would lose weight and start going to the gym and get her life under control.

It was just that all those things seemed a lot easier to achieve after a bottle or two of champagne. It was February already, and her New Year resolutions were still at the talking stage.

She ought at least to have found herself a proper job by now, but nothing was being advertised—no doubt everyone was staying put while they paid off their Christmas credit card bills—and even temping hadn't proved to be the guaranteed fall-back position she had assumed. Nobody seemed to be getting flu this year, and Kate had been about to sign on as a waitress at the local wine bar when Alison had broken her leg.

Tomorrow, Kate told herself. She would buy a paper and check out the appointments page, go to the gym on her way home and cook herself something healthy and non-fattening for supper.

Tomorrow would see the start of the new Kate.

Bella was eating toast in the kitchen with her hair in rollers when Kate let herself into the house. Since Phoebe had married and moved in with Gib, the two of them and Kate's surly cat had had the Tooting house to themselves.

The cat was waiting, a brooding presence by the fridge, and Kate knew better than to try and sit down until he had been fed. He was more than capable of shredding her ankles, so she fished out a packet of the over-priced cat food that was all he would accept and forked

it into his bowl before she had even taken off
her coat.

'I thought you were going out?' she said to
Bella, eyeing the toast enviously.

Bella could eat whatever she liked and still
not put on weight. 'Metabolism,' she said
cheerfully whenever she was challenged by her
less fortunate friends. She was ridiculously
pretty, a blue-eyed blonde with legs that went
on forever and a sunny disposition. The worst
thing about Bella, Kate and Phoebe had often
agreed, was that it was impossible to hate her.

'I am, but Will's taking me to some incred-
ibly cool restaurant where the portions are
bound to be tiny. I thought I'd have something
to eat now so I don't pig out when I get there.
Anyway, I'm hungry,' Bella added simply.

Lucky Bella, going out with the gorgeous
Will while she got some poor old widower
who needed someone to be nice to him. Kate
sighed to herself. Typical.

Without thinking she dropped a slice of
bread into the toaster.

Bella pointed her piece of toast at her.
'You'll regret that,' she warned through a
mouthful. 'Gib always cooks enough for an
army. Anyway, I thought you were on a diet?'

'There's not much point in starting a diet when I'm going out to dinner,' said Kate, taking off her coat at last. 'And we've got to eat up all the fattening food before we can restock with the healthy stuff.'

It was a good enough excuse to slather butter on her toast as she told Bella about borrowing Will mentally. 'I wasn't going to tell Finn McBride that I was just going on a blind date with a sad widower.'

'A widower?'

Kate told her the little she had learnt from Phoebe. 'It doesn't sound like it's going to be a bundle of laughs, does it?'

'Come on, he might be gorgeous,' said Bella.

'Not with my luck,' grumbled Kate, but she did her best to talk herself into a more positive frame of mind as she got ready to go out. Perhaps Bella was right. Perhaps a fabulous hunk of manhood was going to walk into her life tonight and sweep her off her feet. It had to be her turn sometime soon, surely?

Just in case, she dressed carefully in a flounced dress whose plunging neckline showed off her best assets. At least there were some advantages to having a figure like hers. It was just a shame that a curvaceous bust came with equally curvy hips and thighs and tummy.

Wriggling her feet into high heels, she felt instantly taller and therefore better. Kate had often thought that life would be so much easier if only she had slightly longer legs. An extra couple of inches wouldn't have been asking too much now, would it? And a couple less around her hips, which would have balanced her out nicely.

She studied her reflection in the mirror. Amazing what a bit of make-up could do. In a dim light she might even pass for exotic. The warm red in her dress gave her a vaguely gipsyish look that went quite well with her tumbling brown curls and vibrant lipstick. Would the widower be into gipsies? Somehow Kate felt not. Perhaps she should have gone for a rather more demure look?

Could she carry off demure? Kate wondered, unaware that she had lost track of time. It was only when Will arrived to pick up Bella that she thought to look at her watch, and gave a yelp of fright. How could it be eight o'clock already?

It was little comfort to know that Bella wasn't ready either. Will was reading the paper resignedly in the kitchen, and he raised a laconic hand in greeting as Kate teetered down in her heels to ring for a minicab.

'It'll be another twenty minutes,' said the bored voice at the other end of the phone.

Oh, God, now she would be *really* late. Punctuality was another of Kate's New Year resolutions that didn't seem to be working out as planned.

'Sorry, sorry, sorry,' Kate gabbled when she finally arrived at almost quarter to nine, practically falling in the door when Phoebe opened it. 'I know I'm late, but I really didn't mean to be. Please don't be cross with me! It's just been one of those days.'

'It's always one of those days with you, Kate,' said Phoebe, trying to sound severe as she gave her friend an affectionate hug.

Kate hung her head. 'I know, I know, but I am trying to get better.' She lowered her voice conspiratorially. 'Is he here? What's he like?'

'A bit stiff—no, reserved would be a better word,' Phoebe corrected herself. 'But he's very nice when you get to know him, and he's got a lovely smile. I think he's quite attractive, too.'

'Really?' A hot widower after all! Kate perked up. Things were sounding promising. 'No beard?'

'No.'

'Beer belly? Wet lips?'

'No!' Phoebe was laughing now. 'Come and see for yourself.'

Maybe her luck had changed. Smoothing down her top, Kate took a deep breath and followed Phoebe into the sitting room.

'Here's Kate,' she heard her say, but Kate had already stopped dead as she saw who was standing by the mantelpiece with Gib and Josh. He had turned at Phoebe's words, and she had a nasty feeling that his expression of horror only mirrored her own.

It was Finn McBride.

Then he was blocked from her view temporarily as Gib came towards her, grinning. 'Kate!' he cried, sweeping her up into a warm hug. 'Late as usual!'

'I've already grovelled to Phoebe,' Kate said returning his hug and hoping against hope that she had been mistaken and that when Gib moved she would see that the stranger wasn't Finn at all, but just someone who looked like him and either didn't care for the gipsy look or disapproved of unpunctuality. Or both.

But no. Gib was turning with his arm still around her to face the others and there was no doubt about it. There stood Finn, looking as if he had been turned to stone to match the granite of his expression.

Clearly *not* enjoying discovering that he had been set up on a blind date with his own secretary.

Mortified beyond belief, Kate considered her options. Wishing that she had never been born came top of her list, closely followed by that old cliché, a bit tired but effective nonetheless, of wanting the ground to open up and swallow her.

Could she get away with pretending to faint? Probably not, she decided regretfully. She wasn't the fainting type.

Which just left brazening it out.

CHAPTER TWO

'HELLO.' Plastering on an artificially bright smile, she stared Finn straight in the eyes, daring him to acknowledge her. Finn looked back at her with a glacial grey gaze.

'Kate, this is Finn McBride,' said Gib. 'We've been telling him *all* about you.'

Great, thought Kate. Now Finn would know just how sad her life was.

She stuck out her hand and Finn didn't have much choice but to take it. 'Kate Savage,' she introduced herself in a brittle voice, trying not to notice the feel of his fingers closed around hers. In spite of his obvious reluctance, his clasp was firm and warm, much warmer than she had expected, and she snatched her hand away, oddly unsettled.

'You're being very formal, Kate,' said Gib amused. 'At least I don't need to bother introducing you to Josh.' He turned to Finn. 'Josh practically lives with Kate.'

'Oh?' said Finn coldly.

'Kate shares a house with a very good friend of mine,' Josh explained, and the quick smile he gave Kate was sympathetic. He had obviously been told that he was there to make it less obvious that this was a blind date, although his presence wasn't fooling Finn one little bit. 'How are you, Kate? I haven't seen you for a while.'

'I'm fine.' Apart from wanting to die of embarrassment, that was.

Phoebe handed Kate a glass of wine. 'Finn's just been telling us about his disastrous experiences with temps in his office,' she said cheerfully. 'We thought you could give him a few tips on how to handle them.'

Oh, yes, Gib and Phoebe had built her up into a top-flight PA, hadn't they? As if her humiliation wasn't complete enough!

'Really?' Kate produced an acidic smile. 'It does seem to be difficult getting good secretarial staff these days! What's wrong with the temp you've got?'

'She doesn't seem to have any idea of time-keeping for a start,' said Finn with a sardonic glance at the clock on the mantelpiece. No doubt he had been here on the stroke of eight, long before Phoebe and Gib would have been ready for him. 'She's completely unreliable.'

Unreliable, was she? Kate took a defiant gulp of her wine. 'It doesn't sound as if she has much motivation to work for you. Why would that be, do you think?'

Finn shrugged. 'Sheer laziness?' he suggested. 'She seems to have a very vivid fantasy life too,' he went on and Kate coloured in spite of herself, remembering how she was supposed to be sitting here being proposed to right now by a financial analyst called Will.

No doubt Gib and Phoebe had already filled him in on her disastrous relationship with Seb, and even if they hadn't he would still know that story wasn't true either. After all, if she had a financial analyst to go home to, she wouldn't be the kind of sad person who needed to be set up on blind dates by friends.

Kate suppressed a sigh. Could things get any worse?

'It can be just as bad on the other side of fence,' Phoebe was saying loyally. 'Tell them about your horrible boss, Kate. He sounds ghastly.'

Ah. They *could* get worse.

'Oh?' said Finn, thin-lipped. 'Why's that?'

Oh, well. In for a penny, in for a pound. She might as well take the opportunity to tell him what she thought, and it wasn't as if he had spared *her* feelings!

'He's just generally rude and unpleasant,' she told him. 'He doesn't seem to have even the most basic social skills. He can hardly be bothered to say ''good morning'' and as for ''please'' and ''thank you''…well, I might as well ask him to talk Polish!'

A muscle had begun to beat in Finn's jaw. 'Perhaps he's busy.'

'Being busy isn't an excuse for not having any manners,' said Kate, meeting his gaze levelly.

'He's absolute death on personal calls in the office as well,' Phoebe put in, apparently unaware of the antagonism simmering between Finn and Kate. 'Kate's always having to put down the phone in the middle of a conversation when his door opens, and we can be in the middle of a really good chat when she suddenly starts putting on an official voice and telling us she'll get back to us on that as soon as possible. That's our cue to call back later when he's gone! It's very frustrating.'

She turned politely to Finn. 'You let people in your office use the phone, don't you?'

'I don't encourage it, no,' he said with a nasty look at Kate, who was almost beyond caring by now.

She was obviously never going to be able to use the office phone again—not that Kate could imagine going into work again after this. On the scale of embarrassment, being blatantly fixed up with your boss must rank pretty high, she thought. It was certainly one of the most excruciating situations Kate had ever found herself in and, let's face it, she had plenty to compare it to. Sometimes she seemed to spend her life lurching from one mortifying episode to another.

'Access to phones and email for personal business is good for staff morale,' she pointed out. 'If you treated your staff like human beings who have a life outside work, I think you'd see productivity shoot up.'

'There's nothing wrong with our productivity,' snapped Finn, and this time his irritability did catch the others' attention. They looked at him a little curiously and he controlled his temper with an effort.

'There's a difference between dealing with a crisis, in which case of course staff can use the phones, and spending hours gossiping on my time,' he said in a more reasonable voice.

'Doesn't your temp get the job done?' Kate asked sweetly.

'In a fashion,' he admitted grudgingly.

'Perhaps you should go and work for Finn,' said Gib in such a blatant attempt to push them together that he might as well have shown them to the spare room and tucked them in to bed together. 'You might get on better with him than with the boss you've got at the moment.'

'Now, there's an idea!' said Kate as if much struck by the thought. 'Have you got any jobs going at the moment?'

'It's very possible that there might be a vacancy for a temp in my office coming up,' Finn said with something of a snap, 'but that wouldn't interest you, of course, you being such a high-flyer! Gib and Phoebe here were telling me that you practically run the company where you are at the moment. I'm not sure I could offer you anything that challenging.'

A hint of colour touched Kate's cheekbones at his sarcasm. 'No, well, I'm thinking of changing career anyway,' she told him loftily.

'Really?' the other three all said together.

'Yes,' she said, thinking that it wouldn't be such a bad idea, come to that. It didn't look as if she had much future in the secretarial world, anyway. 'I'm sick of being treated like a lower life form, so I've been thinking that I might…what's the word?…downscale.'

'Downscale?' Josh echoed doubtfully, clearly wondering how it was possible for her to downscale from her current position. Being a temp was hardly the giddy heights of a career, was it?

'Or do I mean diversify?' said Kate. 'Do something different anyway. Think out of the box. Use my talents.'

'What exactly are your talents?' Finn asked, the sardonic lift of his brows belying the apparent interest in his voice.

Yes, what *were* her talents? Kate's normally fertile imagination went inconveniently blank at the very moment she needed it most.

'She's a great cook,' Phoebe prompted, evidently still under the impression that Kate might make a suitable wife for Finn.

For some reason it was only at this point that Kate made the connection and remembered that his presence here meant that Finn was a widower. She had been so shocked to see him that she hadn't thought beyond the awkwardness and antagonism, and now she felt suddenly contrite. That beautiful, glowing girl in that photo on his desk was dead. No wonder he seemed so grim.

Kate was conscious of a twinge of guilt about all the times she had thought Finn abrupt and rude, but then, how was she to know that his brusqueness hid a broken heart?

The others were still madly promoting her. 'Kate's a communicator,' she heard Gib say. It was the kind of thing that made you realise just how long he'd spent in the States. 'She's got wonderful people skills.'

'Not just people,' said Josh dryly. 'She's pretty good when it comes to animals too. Remember that dog in the pub, Phoebe?'

'God, yes.' Phoebe gave an exaggerated shudder, and Josh grinned.

'I still wake up in a cold sweat sometimes thinking about it,' he told Finn. 'Kate confronted a skinhead with huge hands and no neck. He was covered in tattoos and snarling and swearing at his dog. Kate told him he wasn't fit to own an animal and took the dog away from him while the rest of us were dancing around in the background being mealymouthed and saying I'm not sure this is a good idea, Kate, why don't you let the RSPCA deal with it? Meanwhile Kate was about half the size of this guy, and giving him a piece of her mind, and the rest of the pub was squaring up for a good fight.'

There was a flicker of interest in Finn's eyes. 'What happened to the dog?'

'Oh, Kate got it,' said Josh. 'We knew she would. It was a savage Alsatian cross, and I wouldn't have wanted to go near it myself, but Kate had it eating out of her hand in no time.' He turned to Kate. 'What *did* happen to that dog?'

'I took him down to my parents,' she said, uncomfortable with all this blatant promotion. 'He's spoiled to death now, of course, and getting much too fat.'

Finn glanced at Kate. 'Do you think the dog really cared one way or another?'

'I don't know,' she said, meeting his eyes defiantly. Why did people like Finn always have to make you feel so stupid and sentimental when it came to animals? 'But someone had to.'

There was a tiny silence.

'A word of warning,' Gib confided to Finn. 'Kate might look sweet and cuddly, but don't ever try mistreating an animal when she's around, or you'll find yourself in big trouble! She's got a hell of a temper when roused.'

Finn's cold grey gaze flicked to Kate, whose cheeks were burning by this stage, and then away. 'I'll remember,' he said.

'What Kate really needs,' said Phoebe as she ushered them all through to the dining room, 'is a house in the country where she can make chutney and keep chickens and dogs and all the other stray people and animals that cross her path.'

'No, I don't,' objected Kate. A big house in the country sounded perfect, but also a bit too much like she was hanging out to get married. She wasn't having Finn thinking that she was desperate for a husband, certainly not desperate enough to consider him!

'I'm a metropolitan chick, really,' she said loftily. 'I don't think I'm ready to make jam yet. I was thinking more along the lines of PR—' She broke off as Phoebe, Gib and Josh burst out laughing, and even Finn managed a sardonic smile. 'What's so funny?' she demanded, offended.

'Kate, darling, you're not nearly tough enough for PR! You'd always side with the underdog regardless of what your client wanted. You might as well decide to be a brain surgeon!'

With that they were off, vying with each other to think up more unlikely careers that Kate could try. Josh's suggestion—pest controller—was voted the best.

'Kate would take all the rats home and make up little beds for them!'

Kate gritted her teeth. She could feel Finn watching her with a curling lip. He was probably one of those people who thought that a soft heart equalled a soft head.

She wouldn't have minded so much if the other three hadn't been so determined to push her as a homemaker. Couldn't they *see* that Finn wasn't the least bit impressed? Things got even worse over dinner when Phoebe manoeuvred the conversation, none too subtly, round to Finn and his daughter.

'What's her name?'

'Alex,' said Finn almost reluctantly.

Kate didn't blame him. He could obviously see the subtext—how much he needed to get married again to provide his daughter with a stepmother—as clearly as she could, and she was conscious of a treacherous twinge of fellow feeling. He couldn't be enjoying this any more than she was.

'She's nine,' he added, evidently recognising that the information was going to be dragged out of him somehow, so he might as well get it over and done with.

'It must have been very hard, bringing her up on your own,' said Phoebe.

Finn shrugged. 'Alex was only two when Isabel died, so I had various nannies to help.

She never really took to any of them, though, and since she's been at school full time we've managed with a housekeeper who comes in every day. She picks Alex up from school and cooks an evening meal, and she'll stay with her if I'm late back from work.'

His voice was emotionless, as if his small daughter was just another logistical problem he had had to solve. It was Alex Kate felt sorry for, poor motherless child. Kate had never taken a phone call from her, or seen her at the office, so she clearly wasn't encouraged to disturb Finn there. Having grown up with four brothers, Kate thought Alex's life sounded very lonely. It couldn't be much fun growing up with just a housekeeper and Finn for company.

Certainly not if Finn was always as boring as he was tonight. He was driving, so he drank very little, and although Kate couldn't object to that, she did feel that he could at least *look* as if was enjoying himself.

He was obviously terrified that she was going to throw herself at him and force him to marry her. It was understandable, Kate supposed, after the way the others had built her up as a domestic goddess, but he needn't worry. Getting together with him was the last thing on her mind. She wasn't *that* desperate for a relationship!

Finn sat beside her at dinner, radiating disapproval as Kate laughed and drank rather too much wine and talked about clubbing and parties and generally made it clear that she was absolutely not in the market for uptight widowers, no matter how sorry she felt for his poor daughter. Of course, the more poker-faced and buttoned up he was, the more she she had to compensate for Phoebe and Gib's sake. They had gone to so much effort, she felt that the least she could do was try and make it a successful evening.

Defiantly ignoring the way Finn was looking down his nose, Kate held out her glass for more wine. Anyone with a sense of occasion would relax and have a drink as well. They would agree to call a taxi and come and pick up the car in the morning, but the Finns of this world evidently didn't do relaxing or having fun.

Of course, it was a bit tricky trying to impress her complete lack of concern on Finn and ignore him at the same time, especially when she was so aware of his austere presence beside her. It wasn't that he didn't contribute to the conversation, but he made it very clear that he thought Kate was too silly for words, which just made her nervous, and nervousness made her drink more until she was trapped in a vicious circle. As the evening wore on, she could hear herself getting louder and more outrageous, and had reached the owlish stage when Finn, obviously unable to bear any more, looked at his watch.

'I must go,' he said, pushing back his chair to forestall any objections.

'I think you should go too,' said Gib to Kate with a grin, 'or you'll never get to work tomorrow.'

Kate didn't want to think about going into work. 'Don't talk about it,' she groaned, closing her eyes, but that was a mistake. The room started to spin and she opened them again hastily, clutching her tousled curls instead.

'I don't suppose you could give her a lift home, could you?' Gib asked Finn. 'She can't be trusted to get home alone in this state!'

'I'm absolutely fine,' Kate protested instantly, lifting her head and trying not to sway at the sudden movement. 'I'm great!'

'You're fab,' agreed Phoebe soothingly, helping her to her feet, 'but it's time to go. Finn's going to take you home.'

'Why can't Josh take me?'

'Because I haven't got my car with me and I live in completely the opposite direction,' said Josh ungallantly.

'I'm very happy to give you a lift,' said Finn with a certain grittiness, clearly feeling far from happy but unable to think of a good excuse.

Outside, it was raining and making a determined effort to sleet, if not actually to snow. Finn watched, resigned, as Gib and Phoebe helped Kate into her coat like a little girl for the short walk to the car, buttoning her up and kissing her goodnight before consigning her into his charge.

Kate thanked them both graciously for supper, although she had a sinking feeling that the words might have come out a bit slurred, and set off down the path, very much on her dignity. Unfortunately, the effect was spoilt by stumbling on her heels, and only Finn's hand which shot out and gripped her arm stopped her landing smack on her bottom.

'Careful!' he said sharply.

'Sorry, the path's a bit slippy…slippery,' Kate managed, wincing at the iron grip of his fingers. She tried to pull her arm away, but Finn kept a good hold of her as he marched her along to his car.

'You're the one that's a bit slippy,' he said acidly and opened the door with what Kate felt was unnecessarily ironic courtesy.

Tired of being treated like a child, she got in sulkily, and he shut it after her with an exasperated click.

The car was immaculate. There were no sweetie wrappers, no empty cans, no forgotten toys or scuffed seats. It was impossible to believe that a child had ever been in it, thought Kate, wondering where poor little Alex fitted into Finn's efficiently streamlined life.

Still buoyed up by a combination of alcohol and nerves, and anticipating an uncomfortable journey, she leant forward and switched on the radio. Classical, of course. Pressing random buttons, she searched for Capital Radio, until Finn got in to the driver's seat and switched it off with a frown.

'Stop fiddling and do up your seatbelt.'

'Yes, sir!' muttered Kate.

Finn lay his arm along the back of her seat and swivelled so that that he could see to reverse the car along the narrow street to the turning place at the bottom. Kate was acutely aware of how close his hand was to her hair and she made a big deal of rummaging in her bag at her feet in case he thought that she was leaning invitingly towards him.

It was a relief when they reached the turning place and Finn took his arm away to put the car into gear. At least she could sit back.

Only it wasn't that much easier then. Finn was a fierce, formidable presence, overwhelming in the dark confines of the car while the rain and the sleet splattered against the windscreen and made the space shrink even further. The light from the dashboard lit his face with a green glow, glancing along his cheekbones and highlighting the severe mouth.

He was concentrating on driving, and Kate watched him under her lashes, daunted more than she wanted to admit by his air of contained competence. It was evident in the calm, decisive way he drove, and when her eyes followed his left hand from the steering wheel to the gear stick, something stirred inside her and she looked quickly away.

Her wine-induced high had shrivelled, leaving her tongue-tied and agonisingly aware of him. It was ridiculous, Kate scolded herself. He was still Finn. He was a disagreeable, if thankfully temporary, boss and an ungracious guest. She didn't like him at all, so why was she suddenly noticing the line of his mouth and the set of his jaw and the strength of his hands?

'Where am I going?'

His brusque question broke the silence and startled her. 'What?'

'Gib asked me to take you home. Presumably he knows where that is, but I'm not a mind-reader.'

'Oh…yes.' Kate huddled in her seat, too appalled by this new awareness of him to rise to his sarcasm the way she would normally have done.

She directed him through the dark streets while the windscreen wipers thwacked rhythmically at the sleety rain and the silence in the car deepened until Kate could bear it no longer.

'Why didn't you tell Gib and Phoebe that you recognised me?'

Finn glanced at her. 'Probably for the same reason that you didn't,' he said curtly. 'I thought it would make the situation even more awkward than it already was.'

His tone was so uninviting, that Kate subsided back into silence. Anyone else giving her a lift home would have made some attempt at conversation, even if only to talk about the evening or the food or even, if things were desperate, the weather, but Finn was evidently in no mood for idle chit-chat. His face was set in grim lines and when he glanced in the rear-view mirror, Kate could see that he was frowning.

'It's just along here.' She pointed out her street in relief. 'There's never anywhere to stop, so if you could drop me here, that would be fine, thanks.'

Finn ignored her, turning down the street she had indicated. 'How far down are you?'

'About halfway,' admitted Kate, surrendering to *force majeure*. She pointed. 'Just past that streetlight.'

As usual, the street was lined with cars bumper to bumper, so Finn had no choice but to stop in the middle of the road. Kate fumbled for the doorhandle as he put on the handbrake.

'Thank you for the lift,' she muttered. 'I hope I haven't brought you too much out of your way.'

A gust of sleet hit her full in the face as she opened the door, and instinctively she recoiled. 'Yuck, what a horrible night!'

'Wait there.' Cursing under his breath, Finn reached behind him for an umbrella and got out of the car. He'd managed to get the umbrella up by the time he made it round to the passenger door. 'I'll see you to your door.'

'Honestly, I'll be fine. You don't need to—'

'Just hurry up and get out!' said Finn through his teeth. It was hard to tell whether they were gritted with temper or with cold. 'The sooner you do, the sooner I can get home!'

Reluctantly Kate scrambled out of the car and into the shelter of the umbrella. The wind was bitter and the rain ran down her neck, but she was still able to notice how intimate it felt to be standing so close to Finn. He was tall and solid and she had a bizarre impulse to put her arms round him and lean into him, to feel how hard and strong he was.

'Right, let's move it before we both freeze to death out here!' said Finn, fortunately unable to read her mind. Or possibly telepathic and quick to take avoiding action. 'Which house is it?'

He set off towards the pavement with Kate teetering on her heels in an effort to keep up with his long stride. 'Why on earth don't you wear something more sensible on your feet?' he demanded, holding the umbrella impatiently above her.

Somehow she got herself out of bed and along to the tube station, but regretted it deeply when she had to stand squashed in with thousands of other commuters, all wet and steaming from the rain above ground. Kate clung to the rail with one hand, swaying nauseously as the train lurched and rattled its way along the tunnels, and tried to ignore the queasy feeling in her stomach.

To make matters worse, her memory of the night before was coming back in fragments of intense clarity separated by the blurry recollection of having generally made a complete fool of herself.

The things she did remember were bad enough. The appalled look on Finn's face when the terrible truth dawned that his date for the evening was none other than his much-despised temporary secretary. The windscreen wipers thwacking in time to the beat of her heart as she fixated inexplicably on his mouth and his hands. Huddling under the umbrella, wondering what it would be like to touch him.

She must have been completely blotto.

God, what if she'd made a pass at Finn? Kate thought in panic. Surely she would remember *that*?

'If I'd known I'd be going on a polar expedition, I might have done!' said Kate, her teeth chattering so loudly that she could hardly speak, but obscurely grateful to the vile weather for disguising the shakiness that might otherwise be obvious in her legs and her voice. She couldn't *believe* what she had been tempted to do just then!

Finn would have had a fit if she had thrown herself at him like that. Or might he, just possibly, have pulled her towards him and kissed her under the umbrella? What would *that* have been like? Kate swallowed, torn between relief and disappointment that she would never know.

Still blissfully unaware of her wayward thoughts, Finn protected her with the umbrella while she fumbled for her key. Her hands were shaking in time with her teeth by that stage, and she was shivering so much that she couldn't get the key in the lock.

Unable to bear it any longer, Finn put out his hand for the key, but his fingers brushing hers were enough to make Kate jerk back in alarm, dropping it into a puddle.

Mortified, she crouched down to retrieve it. Finn was holding out his hand with barely restrained impatience and meekly she dropped the wet and dirty key into his outstretched palm.

Without a word, Finn unlocked the door and pushed it open for her. 'Thank you,' said Kate awkwardly. 'And thanks again for the lift.'

That was Finn's cue to say that it had been a pleasure, an opening he pointedly missed.

'I'll see you tomorrow,' he said gruffly instead.

Fine, if that's the way he wanted to be, she wouldn't invite him in! Kate hugged her coat around her. 'Are you sure you still want me to come into work?'

'That's generally the idea behind paying you,' said Finn with one of his sardonic looks.

'But I thought I was a disaster?'

'You're not exactly a resounding success as a secretary,' he agreed, 'but you're the best I've got at the moment. We've got a big contract coming up, as you would know if you'd been paying attention, and I can't afford to spend the time explaining everything to yet another secretary. I'm better off sticking with you.'

'Well, thanks for that warm vote of confidence!'

'You didn't make many bones about how much you dislike working for me,' Finn

pointed out, 'so I don't see why I should dance around saving your feelings! The fact is that you can't afford to lose this job just yet, and I can't afford the time to replace you.'

'You're saying we're stuck with each other?' said Kate, lifting her chin.

'Precisely, so we might as well make the best of it.' He looked down into her face from under his umbrella. 'I suggest you drink a litre of water before you go to bed,' he said dispassionately as he turned to go. 'We've got a lot to do tomorrow, so please don't be late!'

Groping blearily for the alarm clock, Kate forced open one eye to squint at the time, only to jerk upright with what should have been a cry but which came out more as a groan. The sudden movement was like a cleaver slicing through her aching head and she put up a shaky hand to check that it was still intact.

Unfortunately, yes. Right then death seemed preferable to the pounding in her head and the horrible taste in her mouth.

Not to mention what Finn would say if she was late again.

Kate grimaced as she looked at the clock. If she skipped the shower and was lucky with the trains, she might *just* make it…

If she had, she would have been firmly repulsed. That was one thing she did remember. Her much loved top and favourite shoes had gone down like a lead balloon with Finn. Kate had always been told that she looked really hot in that top, but he had just looked down his nose and averted his eyes from her cleavage. If any pass had been made, it certainly wouldn't have come from him!

She got to the office with less than a minute to spare. Finn was already at his desk, of course. He looked up over his glasses as Kate held on to the doorway for support.

'You look terrible,' he said.

'I feel worse,' she croaked. 'I've got the most monumental hangover.'

Finn grunted. 'I hope you're not expecting any sympathy from me!'

'No, I don't think I could cope with any miracles today,' said Kate tartly before remembering a little too late that her job was very much on the line. Finn was obviously thinking much the same thing because his eyes narrowed slightly behind his reading glasses.

'You'd better be in a fit state to work,' he warned her. 'We've got a lot to do today.'

'I'll just have some coffee and then I'll be fine,' Kate promised, holding her head.

'You can have five minutes,' said Finn and picked up the report he had been reading once more, effectively dismissing her.

Kate groped her way along to the coffee machine and ordered a double espresso, trying not to wince at the sound of ringing telephones and clattering keyboards. There was a tiny manic blacksmith at work inside her skull, banging and hammering on her nerve endings.

Perhaps Alison would have some paracetamol, she thought, sinking gratefully down at her desk. That might help.

Any normal girl would keep hangover cures handy in her top right-hand drawer, but not Alison. Having rummaged through the desk, Kate was forced to accept that Alison didn't have hangovers. Alison probably didn't even know what a hangover *was*. She probably never got nervous or drank too much or showed off in front of Finn.

The coffee was only making her feel worse. Groaning, Kate collapsed onto the desk and buried her head in her arms. That was it. She was giving up. She was just going to have to die here in Finn's office. He would just have to decide what to do with her body although, knowing him, he'd get the next temp to deal with it. Just dispose of that corpse, he would say, and then come in and take notes at the speed of light.

'You didn't drink any water before you went to bed, did you?' Finn's voice spoke above Kate's prostrate form.

'No,' she mumbled, mainly because it was easier than shaking her head.

'You're dehydrated.' Somewhere to the right of her ear, she could hear the sound of a mug being set on the desk. 'Here. I've brought you some sweet tea, and a couple of aspirin.'

The promise of aspirin was enough to make Kate lift her head very cautiously. 'Thanks,' she muttered.

She took the pills and screwed up her face at the taste of the tea, but her mouth was so dry that she sipped it anyway. After a few minutes, she even began to feel as if she might live after all.

Finn was leaning against the edge of her desk, frowning down at the file in his hands. He always seemed to be frowning, Kate thought muzzily. Was he like this with everyone, or was it just her? The thought that it might be her was oddly depressing. Granted, turning up for work late or massively hungover probably wasn't the best way to go about getting him to smile, but still, you'd have thought there'd have been *something* about her he could like.

CHAPTER THREE

As IF aware of her gaze, Finn glanced up. 'Feeling any better?' he asked, although not with any noticeable degree of sympathy.

'A bit,' croaked Kate.

'Good.' Closing the file, he dropped it onto her desk with a loud slap that made her wince, and he sighed. 'Why on earth do you drink so much if you feel this bad the next day?'

'I don't usually,' she said a little sullenly. 'Last night I was trying to have a good time, since *you* obviously weren't going to! Why did you come if you weren't going to make an effort?'

'I went because Gib asked me,' said Finn curtly. 'He said Phoebe had a friend he thought I might like to meet. I was expecting someone gentle and motherly, not a goer with a plunging cleavage, ridiculous shoes and a determination to drink everyone else under the table!'

Aha, so he *had* noticed her cleavage, Kate noted with a perverse sense of satisfaction.

'They've obviously got no idea,' she agreed sweetly, but with an acid undertone. 'They told *me* that you were really nice. How wrong can you be? I don't think I'll be letting them fix up any more blind dates for me!'

A muscle worked in Finn's jaw. 'I couldn't agree with you more.'

'Well, there's a first!' Kate muttered.

Finn got to his feet. 'If you're well enough to argue, you're well enough to do some work,' he said callously. 'I think we can both agree that last night was extremely awkward for both of us. Frankly, I'd rather not know about your personal life, and I don't believe in mixing mine with business. However, as I said last night—although of course you won't remember this!—I can't afford the time to explain everything to someone new at this stage, so I suggest that we pretend that last night never happened and carry on as before. Although it would help if you would turn up on time and in a fit state to work occasionally,' he added nastily. 'That could be different!'

Kate held her aching head with her hand. She just wished she was in a position to tell Finn exactly what he could do with his job. She had a hazy recollection of telling everyone last night that she was planning a major career change, which had seemed like a good idea at the time, and still did, frankly.

One of these days she would have to do something about it but, in the meantime, she had to live, and this crummy job was her best hope of paying her bills for the next few weeks. She had never been big on saving, and she had bailed Seb out too many times to have anything left to fall back on. It looked as if she was going to have to stick with Finn for now.

'Alison should be back in a few weeks,' he said as if reassuring himself.

'Meaning you won't have to put up with me for too long?' In spite of her own reluctance, Kate was obscurely hurt to realise that Finn couldn't wait to get rid of her.

'I was under the impression that the feeling was mutual,' he said coldly.

'It is.'

'Are you trying to tell me you want to leave now?'

'No,' said Kate, forced into a corner. 'No, I want to stay. I haven't got any choice.'

'Then we're both in the same boat,' said Finn. He turned for his office. 'And if you do want to carry on working here, I suggest you go and freshen up, and come back ready to start work!'

Three hours later, Kate was reeling after a barrage of complicated instructions and tasks which Finn rapped out, making no allowances for her hangover, before going out to an expensive lunch with a client.

'Have that draft report on my desk by the time I get back,' was his parting shot.

Kate pulled a face at his receding back and dumped the armful of files and papers onto her desk. Did she really want to hang onto this job that badly?

Finn's expression had been as grimly unreadable as ever, but she could have sworn that beneath it all he was enjoying the sight of her struggling to cope with a hangover and an avalanche of work. She was prepared to bet that a lot of this stuff could easily have waited and that he had only pulled it out to punish her. It was hard to believe that for a peculiar moment or two last night she had actually found him attractive!

Running her fingers wearily through her hair, Kate sighed as she contemplated the scattered piles of paper on her desk. She needed another coffee before she could tackle that lot!

In spite of everything Finn had to say about his staff not going in for gossip, Kate had noticed that the coffee machine was a favoured meeting place. Of course it was possible that the two older women from the finance department were talking about work, but somehow she doubted it. They stopped as she approached and moved aside politely to let her through to the machine.

'Thanks,' said Kate with a smile. 'I'm desperate!'

'Feeling rough?'

'Awful,' she admitted, searching her memory for their names. 'I am never, ever, going to drink again!'

Elaine and Sue, that was it. They had been polite if rather cool with Kate in her few brief dealings with them, but she noticed they thawed slightly at her frank admission of a hangover.

'So, how are you getting on?' the older one—Sue?—asked.

'I don't think I'm ever going to live up to Alison's standards,' Kate sighed as the machine spat out coffee into her cup. 'What's she like? Is she as perfect as Finn makes out?'

Sue and Elaine considered. 'She's certainly very efficient,' said Elaine, but she didn't sound overly enthusiastic. 'Finn relies on her a lot.'

Kate sipped her coffee, still disgruntled by the amount of work Finn had thrown at her.

'She must be an absolute saint to put up with him!'

Wrong thing to say! The two women bridled at the implied criticism of Finn. 'He's lovely when you get to know him,' Elaine insisted, and Sue nodded.

'He's the best boss I've ever had. You want to count how many people have been here years and years. We don't get the same kind of turnover as in other companies. That's because everyone here feels involved. Finn expects you to work hard, but he always notices and comments on what you've been doing, and that makes all the difference.'

'He treats you like a human being,' Elaine added her bit.

It was news to Kate, thinking about that morning.

'Of course, Alison's absolutely devoted to Finn,' Sue said. She lowered her voice confidentially. 'Between you and me, I think she might be hoping to become more than a PA one day.'

'Oh?' Kate was conscious of a sudden tightening of her muscles. 'Do you think that's likely?'

'No.' Elaine shook her head definitely. 'He's never got over losing his wife, and I don't think he ever will.'

'Isabel was a lovely person,' Sue agreed. 'She used to come in to the office sometimes, and we all loved her. She was so beautiful and sweet and interested in what everyone did. There was just something about her. She made you feel special somehow, didn't she, Elaine?'

Elaine nodded sadly. 'Finn was different then. He absolutely adored her, and she was the same. She used to light up whenever he came into the room. Oh, it was such a tragedy when she died!'

'What happened?' asked Kate, hoping she didn't sound too ghoulish.

'Someone got into a car having had too much to drink, and poor Isabel was coming the other way...' They shook their heads at the memory of it. 'She never came out of the coma. Finn had to make the decision to switch off her life-support machine.'

Sue sighed. 'You can only imagine what it was like for him. He had Alex to worry about too. She was in the car as well, so she was in hospital too, although not so seriously hurt.'

'She wasn't much more than a baby,' Elaine added. 'Just old enough to cry for her mummy.'

Kate's hand had crept to her mouth as she listened to their story. 'That's…terrible,' she said, feeling hopelessly inadequate.

'Terrible,' Elaine agreed. 'Finn's never been the same since. He closed in on himself after Isabel died. Alex is his life now, and he won't let anyone else close. He kept the company going, but I've always felt that was more for all the staff here than for his own sake.'

'We all hope he'll remarry one day,' Sue said. 'He deserves to be happy again and Alex needs a mum. Maybe he'll miss Alison while she's away,' she added hopefully. 'I know she can be a bit cool, but that's just her manner, and she's very attractive, isn't she?' she demanded of Elaine, who nodded a bit reluctantly.

'She's always beautifully groomed.'

'And she must know him pretty well after working for him for so long. I think she'd be a good wife for him.'

It didn't sound to Kate as if Alison was at all the right kind of wife for Finn. He was quite cool and efficient enough by himself. What he needed was warmth and tenderness and laughter, not practicality and good grooming.

Not that it was anything to do with her, of course.

Still, she couldn't get Finn's tragic story out of her mind all afternoon. She kept imagining him by his wife's side, with the life-support machines beeping in the background, willing her to open her eyes, or trying to explain to his baby daughter why her mother couldn't come.

'No wonder he didn't approve of me drinking last night,' she said to Bella that evening, having told her about the disaster of her blind date and what she had learnt from Elaine and Sue. 'I feel terrible now. I've been so nasty about him, and all the time he's had to cope with all of that.'

'Don't do it,' said Bella, handing Kate a drink.

'Don't do what?'

'Don't get involved.'

'I'm not involved,' said Kate a little defensively. 'I just feel desperately sorry for him.'

Bella sighed as she contemplated her friend. 'You know what you're like, Kate,' she warned. 'One tiny tug at your heartstrings, and you're turning your world upside down to try and make things better, and sometimes you just can't. You were desperately sorry for Seb, too, and look where that got you!'

'This is entirely different,' Kate protested. 'Finn's not trying to get anything from me. He hasn't even told me about Isabel himself. I'm not sure he'd even want me to know.'

'I just don't want you jumping from feeling sorry for him to wanting to help him to falling in love with him,' said Bella with a warning look. 'You've got to admit it's a bit of a pattern with you, and this time you really could get hurt. It would be much worse than Seb. You'd never be able to live up to a perfect wife like that, Kate. You'd only ever be second-best.'

'Honestly, Bella!' said Kate crossly. 'Anyone would think I was planning to marry him! All I'm saying is that maybe I should be more understanding when he's grumpy with me.'

'Hhmmnn, well, just be careful. You didn't like him when you thought he was happily married, and he's exactly the same man. Being a widower isn't really an excuse for being unpleasant to you, is it? You said it's six years since his wife died, that's long enough for him to be coming to terms with it. Don't let him take advantage of your soft heart, that's all.'

Kate didn't say any more—*ER* was on, and there were more important things to do—but afterwards she thought about what Bella had said. Her friend might seem the quintessential feather-headed blonde at times, but she could be very pragmatic when it came to relationships.

Of course, it was nonsense to suggest that there was any chance of her falling in love with Finn. She had no intention of doing anything of the kind. What she *would* do from now on was make allowances for his brusque temper instead of getting cross about it.

It would be part of her new, professional image, Kate decided. She would be cool, courteous and discreetly efficient. If all she could do to help him was to create a calm atmosphere in which he could work, then that's what she would do.

That was nothing like falling in love with him, was it?

Changing the atmosphere in the office was all very well in theory, but in practice it was less easy.

Kate really tried. Sick of hearing about the immaculately groomed Alison, she had made more of an effort to dress smartly. She was never going to look completely at home in a suit and her hair just didn't do neat, but at least she was showing willing. When Finn snapped at her, she bit her tongue and didn't answer back. She just got on with her work and waited for him to notice how much easier his life had become. She even practised an understanding speech for when he told her how grateful he was.

That was a waste of time! Far from being grateful, Finn seemed deeply suspicious of her new, improved attitude.

'What's the matter with you?' he demanded.

'Nothing,' said Kate, a bit taken aback.

'You're too polite,' he grumbled. 'It makes me nervous. And why are you dressed like that?' His expression sharpened. 'Have you got an interview for another job?'

Chance would be a fine thing. 'No,' she said. 'I'm just trying to look professional. I thought you would approve,' she was unable to resist adding.

Finn looked at her. Her attempt to tie back her hair had failed miserably, most of the soft brown curls escaping their confines to tumble around her face once more. Her one and only suit was a rather dull grey affair and the white shirt was creased. It was hard to believe they came from the same wardrobe as the vibrant dress with its swirling skirt and its daring neckline that she had worn to dinner at Phoebe and Gib's.

'I'm not sure you can carry off the professional look,' he said dryly.

There was no pleasing some people, thought Kate with an inward sigh.

Faced with a comprehensive lack of encouragement on Finn's part, she found herself slipping back into her old ways, especially after an interesting little chat with Phoebe one evening. Kate had braced herself to confess that she had known exactly who Finn was, and was a little peeved to discover that Finn had told Gib himself the very next day when he had rung to thank them for supper.

'Did he say anything about me?' Kate heard herself ask when Phoebe had finished telling her how amused they were by the whole situation.

'I think he was a bit thrown by seeing you dressed like that,' said Phoebe, carefully avoiding a direct answer. 'Presumably you don't usually wear quite such revealing tops in the office?'

'Of course not,' said Kate, miffed for no obvious reason. 'What was he expecting? Me to turn up to dinner in a suit?'

'I gather Finn told Gib that I wasn't his type,' she said when she reported the conversation to Bella.

She was cross that she hadn't spoken to Phoebe earlier so that she could have passed a message onto Finn that he wasn't Kate's type either.

'I don't think I'll bother being nice to him any longer,' she grumbled. 'He obviously doesn't appreciate it anyway.'

Still, that was no reason to give up her new cool image. Kate was determined to show Finn that Alison wasn't the only one who could be professional. Every morning she tried to be at her desk before he arrived, calmly going through the post. It meant getting up at the crack of dawn, of course, but it was worth it to see the disconcerted look on his face when he came in, and it wasn't as if she would have to do it for ever. She fully intended to go back to her slovenly ways the moment Alison returned.

She was nearly a week into her newly punctual mode when she emerged from the underground one day, turning up her collar against the cold. It was a dreary morning, with a sleety drizzle giving the pavements a slippery sheen, and Kate paused to put up her umbrella.

Normally she wouldn't have bothered, but the rain made her hair even more uncontrollable than ever, and she was determined to achieve a style that would stay halfway neat for the morning at least.

She glanced at her watch. Just time to get a cappuccino from the Italian café on the way to the office.

Kate stood in line with all those others unable to face another revolting coffee from the machine at work. Accepting a perfunctory *'Bella, bella!'* from the Italian as he handed her the beaker to take away, she cradled it close to her chest for warmth. She would really enjoy this when she was sitting calmly at her desk, waiting for Finn to appear.

Putting up the umbrella with one hand turned out to be a tussle of wills, but after some wrestling, Kate won. It was raining more heavily now, and the wind was coming in gusts, so she had to hold the umbrella almost in front of her face to stop it blowing inside out. It made it tricky to see where she was going, but she set off, telling herself that there was only a block to the office. She might as well try and stay dry.

The next moment there was a yelp and she was sprawling full length, her fall partly cushioned by a pile of rubbish bags waiting to be collected.

'Are you all right?' someone stopped to ask reluctantly.

'I'm fine...I think,' said Kate, struggling to her feet and looking down at herself as she brushed the rubbish off her jacket in dismay. The cappuccino had ended up all the way down her skirt. Her hands were filthy, her tights torn, and as for her hair...well, she might as well forget it for today.

Relieved at not being roped into a scene, her reluctant Samaritan had hurried on. Kate bent stiffly to retrieve her umbrella, remembering the yelp and wondering what had caused it. She could see now that some of the pile of black bags had been torn open, so that rubbish spilt out onto the pavement, and in the middle of them, cowered a little dog with bony ribs and fearful eyes.

Her bruises forgotten, Kate crouched down among the bin bags and held out her hand. 'You poor sweetheart, did I tread on you?' she asked gently, holding out her hand, until the dog crawled closer to lick it. It was wet and shivering, and when Kate looked closer she could see that it had no collar.

'You're not much more than a puppy, are you?' she said, letting it smell that she was unthreatening before she stroked it behind its ears, one of which was cocked and the other flapping disreputably.

It was not perhaps the most beautiful dog she had ever seen. A dispassionate observer might even have thought it was ugly with its legs disproportionately short in relation to its long shaggy body, its pointed, whiskery nose and big ears, but Kate saw only the thinness of its ribs and the untreated sores, and her blood boiled.

There was no point in looking round for an owner. This was a business district, the streets lined with office blocks and no one would be walking a dog around here. This little dog wasn't lost, it had been abandoned, if indeed it had ever had a home in the first place. But something in the way its tail wagged feebly in response to her gentle pats made Kate's heart crack.

'Come on, darling, you're coming with me,' she told it firmly. She couldn't leave it here to starve if it didn't get run over first.

Very gently, she pulled the little dog towards her. It whimpered but didn't struggle when she lifted it up. When she examined it, it didn't seem to be badly hurt. 'I think you're just cold and hungry,' she decided.

There was a mini-market back by the tube station. Tucking the now useless umbrella under one arm and the dog under the other, Kate retraced her steps and bought some bread and milk, and a couple of newspapers in case of accidents. She would have to worry about a lead and collar later. This wasn't the kind of area you found a pet shop, even if she had time to track one down. By this stage she was almost as dirty and bedraggled as the little dog, and it was nearly half past nine.

So much for being early.

Well, it couldn't be helped. Ignoring the receptionist's appalled expression, Kate walked towards the lift with the precious burden under her arm. She could feel its little heart battering and her own didn't feel that steady at the prospect of facing Finn, but she was still too angry at the cruelty of anyone who could abandon a defenceless animal to care what she looked like.

The door of her office was open. Kate took a deep breath and walked inside, only to stop dead when she saw that there was someone sitting at her computer. For a heart-stopping moment she thought that she had been replaced, but a second look showed her that the occupier of her desk had quite a bit of schooling left before she had to think about getting a job.

The little girl stopped typing when Kate came in and stared at her with unfriendly eyes. She had thick glasses and a thin, guarded face, together with an air of self-possession quite intimidating in one so young.

'Who are you?'

'I'm Kate. Who are you?' countered Kate, although she had already recognised that steely expression. Like father, like daughter.

'Alex,' she admitted. 'My dad's angry with you,' she went on.

'Oh, dear, I was afraid he might be.' Kate put the little dog down and stroked it soothingly.

'He said a rude word.'

That sounded like Finn. 'Where is he now?'

'He's gone to find someone to look after me and to fill in for you until you deign to turn up,' said Alex, obviously quoting verbatim. 'What does "deign" mean?'

'I think your father thought I was late on purpose,' said Kate, sighing. She took off her jacket and hung it up while she wondered what to do next. She really ought to find Finn and explain, but the little dog was still shivering with a combination of nerves and cold.

She knew how it felt.

Alex had been studying her critically. 'Why are you so dirty?'

'I fell into a load of rubbish.'

'Yuck.' Alex wrinkled her nose. 'You do smell a bit,' she informed Kate, who lifted an arm and sniffed the unmistakable odour of rotting rubbish. Eau de bin bag.

Great. That was all she needed.

Alex had come round the front of the desk and was regarding the quivering dog with some wariness. 'Is that your dog?'

'He is now,' said Kate.

'What's his name?'

'I don't know…what do you think I should call him?'

'Is it a boy or a girl?'

Good question. Kate lifted the dog gently. 'A boy.'

Alex came a little closer. She seemed cautious but fascinated by the dog, who was sniffing the floor with equal uncertainty. Kate waited for her to suggest Scruffy or Patch or Rover.

'What about Derek?'

'*Derek*?' Kate started to laugh, and Alex looked offended.

'Don't you think it's a good name?'

'It's a great name,' Kate recovered herself quickly. 'Derek the dog. I love it. Derek!' she called to the dog, snapping her fingers for his attention.

He pricked up his ears and sat down clumsily, which made Alex smile for the first time. Her smile transformed her rather serious little face, and Kate wondered if a smile would have a similar effect on Finn's expression.

Not that she was likely to see him smile just for the moment.

Alex squatted beside her. 'Hello, Derek,' she said.

'Let him smell your fingers before you pat him,' said Kate, and smiled when Derek wagged his tail and licked Alex's hand.

'He's cute,' said Alex.

'I'm not sure your father will think so.'

The words were barely out of her mouth before Finn came striding into the room, scowling ferociously. 'Oh, there you are!' he said as he spied Kate. 'Nice of you to join us!'

Kate got to her feet, acutely conscious of her bedraggled state. 'I'm sorry I'm late,' she began but Finn interrupted her as he got a proper look at her.

'For God's sake, Kate, look at the state of you! What on earth have you been doing?'

'Please don't shout!' she said, but it was too late. Cowering at the sound of Finn's raised voice, the little dog had squatted and made a puddle on the carpet.

'Now look what you've done!' Kate accused Finn as she pulled one of the newspapers apart and spread a couple of sheets over the puddle to mop up the worst of it. 'It's all right, sweet-heart,' she said, caressing the still trembling dog. 'I won't let the nasty man shout at you any more.'

She glanced up at Finn from where she was crouched. 'You're upsetting Derek.'

'Upsetting…?' Finn shook his head in baffled frustration. 'Who?'

'It's his name, Dad,' Alex told him.

'*Derek*?'

'Alex thought of the name,' said Kate quickly, before he could say anything to upset his daughter. 'It suits him, don't you think?'

Finn ignored that. He looked as if he was counting to ten in an effort to keep his temper. 'Kate,' he said at last in a voice of careful restraint, 'what is that dog doing here?'

'I found him on my way to work.'

'Well, you'd better lose him pretty damn quickly! An office is a totally inappropriate place for a dog.'

'It's not that appropriate for a child either.'

His mouth thinned. 'That's a completely different thing,' he snapped. 'My housekeeper has been called away unexpectedly to look after her sick mother, and the school is having a training day. I didn't have any choice but to bring Alex in today. I couldn't leave her in the house on her own.'

'I couldn't leave Derek in the street on his own,' countered Kate. 'He would have been run over.'

Finn ground his teeth in frustration. 'Kate, this is an office, not Battersea Dogs Home! I thought you were trying to be more professional?'

'Some things are more important than being professional,' she said, and bent to pick up the dog.

'Where are you going?' he snarled. 'I haven't finished with you!'

'I'm going to dry him and give him something to drink,' Kate answered patiently, 'and when I've done that, I'll come back and you can be as cross with me as you like.'

'Can I come and help you?' Alex asked while her father was still spluttering in outrage.

'Sure,' said Kate. 'You can hold Derek while I dry him.'

'Now just a minute—' Finn began, unable to believe that he had lost control of the situation so easily.

Alex rolled her eyes in an impressively adolescent fashion. 'Dad, I'll be fine,' she said wearily, and followed Kate out of the room before he could assert his authority.

In the Ladies, they found some paper towels and wiped the worst of the dirt and wet off Derek, and then off Kate, who was in nearly as bad a state.

She pulled a face at her reflection as she washed her hands. 'I don't think I'm going to win any awards for glamour today,' she sighed.

Alex was cuddling the little dog, murmuring to reassure it about finding itself in yet more strange surroundings. 'You're not like Alison,' she commented.

Kate sighed and lifted her hopelessly tangled hair in despair. 'So your father is always telling me.'

'I don't like Alison,' Alex confided. 'She talks to me in a stupid voice like I'm a baby! She's soppy about Dad, too.'

'Is your dad soppy about her?' Kate couldn't help asking, although she knew that she shouldn't. She hoped she didn't sound too interested.

Alex shrugged. 'I don't know. I hope not. I don't want a stepmother. Rosa fusses, but I'd rather have her as a housekeeper than Alison.'

Poor old Alison, thought Kate. There was a very stubborn set to Alex's chin, inherited from her father no doubt, and she wouldn't like to bet on Alison's chances of winning her round.

Feeling more cheerful for some reason, she sent Alex in search of a couple of bowls while she made a bed of newspapers for Derek behind her desk where he would feel secure. He seemed quite happy to curl up there, but when Alex reappeared with a bowl of water and a saucer, he got up to investigate, and the offer of some bread soaked in milk got his tail wagging eagerly.

'He's so sweet!' said Alex, watching him adoringly. 'I wish I could keep him! Do you think Dad would let me?'

Kate thought the answer would be definitely not, but Finn could presumably deal with his own daughter. 'You'd have to ask him. I'd wait until he's in a better mood though,' she cautioned.

This looked like good advice when Finn emerged glowering from his office. 'Alex, you can go and sit with the girls at the reception desk for a while if you want. You know you like doing that sometimes.'

'Only when Alison is here,' muttered Alex. 'Anyway, I'm going to look after Derek. Kate says I can.'

'Yes, well, I want a word with Kate,' said Finn ominously.

'I won't disturb her,' Alex reassured him, misunderstanding. 'It'll make it easier for her to work because she won't have to check on Derek the whole time. You don't mind, do you, Kate?'

'It's fine by me.'

'It's not a question of what Kate minds,' Finn bit out, goaded beyond endurance. 'Come into my office,' he ordered Kate. 'If you've quite finished turning my office into a branch of Animal Rescue, that is,' he added sarcastically, standing back with mock courtesy so that she could go ahead of him.

'Would you like to explain what the hell is going on?' he said furiously as he sat behind his desk.

Kate wondered if she was supposed to stand in front of him with her hands behind her back, like being brought before the headmaster. She opted to sit anyway. Finn was so angry that one more thing wasn't going to make any difference. He certainly couldn't look any crosser.

'Nothing's going on,' she told him. 'I didn't mean to be late, but I couldn't just walk past that dog. You saw the state of him. Someone's just got bored of him and thrown him out. I don't know how people can be so cruel.' Her voice shook with emotion.

'They should bring back public flogging,' added Kate, who rescued spiders and stepped carefully round snails and loathed all forms of violence. 'That might teach them what cruelty feels like! I once saw—'

Finn cut her off. 'Kate, I'm not interested,' he said curtly. 'I've got a business to run here. It's distracting enough having to cope with Alex in the office, and now we've wasted half the morning on that dog.'

'Alex is quite happy looking after him, so I'd say that's solved your problem. In fact, it's all worked out very well,' said Kate, unrepentant. She waved her notebook at him and smiled brightly. 'I'm ready to start work whenever you are.'

CHAPTER FOUR

'DAD?' Alex waited until Finn had finished giving Kate a long list of orders which she was scribbling into her notebook.

Finn peered round the desk to where his daughter sat in the corner, Derek's head on her lap. 'Are you OK down there?'

She nodded vigorously. 'You know you said that I could have whatever I wanted for lunch if I was good this morning?'

'Yes,' he said with a certain wariness.

'I don't really want any lunch,' she told him. 'Can we go to a pet shop and buy Derek a lead and collar instead?'

'Alex, I don't want you getting too attached to that dog!'

'No, I won't,' she promised fervently. 'But please, Dad! You did promise.'

'I was thinking more of going out for a pizza.' Finn glared at Kate as if it was all her fault. 'Perhaps we should let Kate take responsibility for the dog. She rescued it, after all.'

'Kate hasn't got time to go out to lunch,' said Alex before Kate had a chance to speak.

How true, thought Kate, looking at her list. She had just been thinking that she would need to improvise a lead and collar. 'I'm sure I'll be able to find some string or something,' she said, opting for the martyr approach which she was fairly sure would annoy Finn. 'You go out and enjoy your lunch. Don't worry about me.'

Finn scowled. 'Oh, yes, that's going to do wonders for our professional image, isn't it? My PA leaving the office with a dog on a piece of string!'

'I can wait until everyone else has gone,' Kate offered innocently.

'Oh, Dad, please say we can go to a pet shop,' Alex interrupted. 'I've been good— haven't I, Kate? And you did say just the other day that everyone should keep their promises.'

Kate suppressed a smile as Finn champed in frustration. Alex clearly needed no advice in managing her father.

'I don't know where we're going to find a pet shop in the middle of London,' he grumbled, but he had obviously given in on the point of principle.

'Most of the big department stores should have a pet department,' said Kate helpfully.

Not that Finn looked very grateful.

When Alex had gone off with her father, the dog crept closer to Kate, wriggling ingratiatingly. Really he wasn't very beautiful, but his liquid brown eyes were so trusting that her heart melted.

She knew that she shouldn't let herself get too attached to him either. She couldn't keep him and would have to find him a good home somewhere else but, still, she lifted him up, unable to resist the appeal of that tail. He was small enough to sit on her lap, where he licked her hands and curled up comfortably.

To hell with professionalism, Kate decided. It wasn't as if he was stopping her working. She could still type and email and make phone calls.

It was nearly half past two by the time Finn and Alex returned, laden with basket, toys, bowls, a pooper scooper, and dog food, as well as the lead and collar that had been the ostensible purpose of the exercise. Kate quickly put Derek on the floor before Finn spotted him.

He—Finn, not the dog—wore a resigned expression as Alex proudly showed Kate what she had persuaded her father to buy.

'Here's his collar,' she said, producing it with a flourish.

Kate couldn't help laughing when she saw it. It was made of red velvet and studded with mock diamonds, the kind of nonsense that cost a fortune.

'Don't tell me!' she said. 'Your dad chose this!'

The irony went over Alex's head, but Kate saw the corner of Finn's mouth twitch, and felt as if she had conquered Everest. OK, it wasn't exactly a smile, but it was a response.

She forced her attention back to Alex, who was assuring her that it was a present. 'I used my own money,' she said proudly.

'That's very nice of you,' said Kate, looking doubtfully at the pile of goodies for Derek. Alex must have a very generous allowance.

'Dad paid for the rest,' Alex admitted, almost as if she had read her mind.

Kate glanced at Finn. That tantalising glimpse of humour had vanished, leaving him aloof and austere once more. 'I'll write you a cheque,' she promised.

'Please don't,' he said. 'I'd rather forget the whole business as soon as possible. I can think of better ways to spend a lunch hour than trailing around the pet department being subjected to emotional blackmail by a nine-year-old!'

'Well, thank you anyway,' said Kate, deciding to make it up to him somehow later. She stooped to fasten the collar around Derek, who shook himself at the unfamiliar feel of it. 'Look how smart you are now!' she told him, and smiled at Alex. 'It *was* kind of you to give up your lunch for him.'

'I had a pizza as well,' Alex had to admit.

Kate laughed, even as her own stomach rumbled with hunger. 'I didn't think your dad would let you go hungry.'

'Look, we brought you a sandwich,' said Alex to her surprise, taking a bag from her father. 'Dad said you needed some lunch.'

Kate peered into the bag to find half a baguette temptingly stuffed with chicken and bacon and avocado. All of her favourite things in fact. How on earth had he known?

She lifted her eyes to meet Finn's, and something shifted in the air between them. 'Thank you,' she said, ridiculously breathless.

'I can't afford to have you passing out from hunger,' he said gruffly. 'We've still got a lot to do this afternoon.'

Still, he had thought of her. A little thrill went through Kate at the knowledge, at least until she managed to suppress it. Letting herself feel little thrills like that about Finn would be bad, bad, bad, and Bella's voice seemed to echo in her ears. *Don't do it, Kate.*

She moistened her lips and handed him a folder of letters for him to sign. 'I've made those appointments you wanted, and the final draft of the tender is being copied right now.'

'And the arrangements for next Thursday?'

'Yes, they're done.'

'You've been busy,' he grunted, and in spite of everything Kate felt herself warm at his grudging approval.

Oh, dear, careful, Kate, she warned herself.

She was busy all afternoon, and in the end Finn arranged for one of the girls from reception to go with Alex when she wanted to take Derek for a little walk. The rest of the time the little girl was quite happy to play with him and the two of them spent hours chasing balls up and down the corridor, but by five o'clock they were both flagging.

Kate knocked on Finn's door. 'I think Alex needs to go home,' she said, bracing herself for him to tell her to mind her own business. 'I'll stay and finish up here if you want to go.'

Finn looked at his watch and frowned. 'I didn't realise the time. Yes, I'd better take her home.' He glanced at Kate. 'Are you sure?'

'Yes. I owe you extra time anyway after I was late this morning. Then we can call it quits,' she suggested. 'I don't mind staying, honestly. I don't want to take the dog home in the rush hour, and anyway, there's not that much more to do.'

'Well...thanks,' said Finn roughly as he got to his feet and shrugged on his jacket. He sounded deeply uncomfortable and Kate guessed that he didn't like having to be grateful to anyone for anything.

'It's nothing,' she said, brushing it aside. 'I'm sorry for all the hassle I've caused.'

Finn was patting his pockets for his keys. 'What are you going to do about that dog?' he asked abruptly as Kate turned for the door.

'My parents live in the country. They love animals and they've got lots of space, so I'm sure they'd take him, but they're away on holiday at the moment, and won't be back for a few weeks. I'll keep him with me in the meantime.'

She chewed her lip as she considered what it would mean. 'It would mean leaving him all day, but I could walk him as soon as I got home—unless I could bring him to the office with me?' She looked at Finn hopefully. 'He wouldn't be any trouble. You've seen how quiet he is.'

Right on cue came the sound of excited barking and Alex's laugh. Finn looked at Kate.

'Normally,' she added.

Finn sighed. 'I think Alex is going to be more of a problem than the dog. She won't want to be separated from it now.'

He was right. Alex was adamant that Derek should go home with her. 'He's just got used to me,' she protested. 'He'll be confused if I leave him now.'

'You trust me to look after him, don't you?' said Kate, trying to defuse the imminent stand-off between Finn and his daughter.

'It's not that.' Alex's bottom lip stuck out mutinously. 'If I can't take him home, I won't see him again, and I want to keep him,' she wailed. 'Please, Dad! You know I've always wanted a dog.'

Finn raked his fingers through his hair in frustration. 'Alex, you know it's not possible for you to look after a dog. You're at school all day.'

'Rosa wouldn't mind looking after him during the day.'

'I'm not so sure about that, and anyway, Rosa's not there, so we can't ask her at the moment.'

The bottom lip wobbled. 'But what's going to happen to him?'

Patiently, Finn explained that Kate would look after the dog until she could take it down to her parents.

'Well, couldn't I keep him until then?' pleaded Alex desperately.

'He'll still need a walk during the day, Alex.'

Alex pounced on the flaw in her father's argument. 'How is Kate going to walk him then? She's at work longer than I'm at school.'

Finn gritted his teeth at the realisation that he had been boxed into a corner. He was going to have to give in to one of them. 'Kate's going to bring him into the office,' he said, succumbing to the inevitable.

'Then why couldn't you bring him in, Dad?' Alex persisted. 'You've got a car, so it wouldn't make any difference to you. I'd walk him in the morning and in the evening when you bring him home, and he could spend the day with you.'

Finn cast a meaningful look at Kate. It was crystal clear that he thought that it was her dog and her responsibility to knock the idea on its head once and for all. Kate met his eyes with a bland smile. She was rather enjoying seeing Finn comprehensively out-argued by a nine-year-old.

'I think that's a good idea,' she said, wilfully ignoring her cue and Finn's baleful glare. 'I could walk him at lunch time so your dad doesn't have to be bothered with him,' she offered to Alex, whose face brightened instantly.

'Oh, yes, *please!*'

'And what happens when Alison comes back?' demanded Finn, annoyed at being out-manoeuvred. 'She might not feel like walking a dog in her lunch break!'

Alex barely missed a beat. 'Rosa's mother might be better then and she can come back. I bet she wouldn't mind Derek.'

Kate suppressed a smile at Finn's expression. 'You've done a wonderful job of bringing Alex up,' she told him with mock seriousness. 'Not many girls of nine could argue so well! You must be very proud of her.'

'I don't think I'd choose proud to describe the way I'm feeling right now,' said Finn, exasperated, but it was obvious that he had decided that he was fighting a losing battle.

'Very well,' he said, turning back to his daughter. 'But—'

He was interrupted by Alex throwing herself into his arms with a shriek of delight. 'Oh, thank you, thank you, thank you!' she cried, almost drowned out by Derek who went into a frenzy of shrill barking as he picked up on the excitement.

For a moment, there was chaos, and Kate couldn't help laughing. At the same time she couldn't help being touched by the way Finn hugged his daughter back. He might hide behind a gruff exterior but it was obvious that they adored each other.

Kate even felt a little bit excluded, which of course was ridiculous. *She* didn't want to be gathered up and hugged and included in their little family unit with the dog. She was supposed to be a hip metropolitan chick, not yearning for security and love, right?

Right.

'*But*—' Finn managed to raise his voice above the commotion at last. 'On one condition. You're not to get too attached to this dog, Alex. You're at school, I'm at work, and it's not part of Rosa's job to walk a dog. You can take him home with you now, but only as long as Kate is working here, or until she can take him to her parents. That's the deal. OK?'

Alex looked up at him speculatively. Kate could practically hear her thinking that this was the best offer she was going to get for now, so she might as well accept and find another plan for when the first one came to an end.

'OK,' she said, and looking at the tilt of her chin, so like her father's, Kate thought that Finn was probably going to end up having a dog whether he wanted it or not.

Kate herself thought it had worked out pretty well. Her parents would take Derek, of course, but she didn't really want to ask them again, having landed them with so many other waifs and strays in the past. She wished she could keep Derek, but it was hopeless when you were temping and, anyway, she could already see the bond that existed between the dog and the little girl. Derek would be happier with Alex.

'I hope Alison never comes back,' Alex whispered when Finn went to get his coat, and Kate was disconcerted to realise that she didn't want Alison to come back either.

The next morning it was Finn's turn to be late. He came into the office with Derek prancing and chewing on his lead, to find Kate sitting behind her desk and looking innocently at her watch.

'Don't say anything!' he warned her, unamused.

Kate grinned. 'I wasn't going to.'

'I suppose you realise that you and this dog between you have completely disrupted my life?' grumbled Finn, letting Derek go as he recognised his saviour of the day before and went into frenzy of excitement.

Released, he dashed over to Kate, who picked him up, still wriggling ecstatically, but then had to turn her head away from his attempts to lick her cheek and chin, her face lit with laughter.

The suit had had to go to the cleaners after yesterday's encounter with a pile of rubbish, so she was back to wearing a long skirt in some vaguely ethnic pattern with a top that clung to her curves and was, in spite of its long sleeves and high neck, somehow much more disturbing than the more revealing one she had worn to dinner at Phoebe and Gib's.

She had given up on her hair as well, and it fell in soft brown curls to her shoulders. To Finn she looked vaguely scruffy but startlingly warm and vivid as she stood there with the squirming dog in her arms against the background of sterile office equipment.

'That dog is completely out of control,' he said, his voice very dry as if his throat was tight.

'Oh, but he's so sweet! How could he possibly be any trouble?'

'Have you ever tried taking him for a walk? He's got no idea how to walk on a lead and if you let him off he goes round in manic circles or runs off and won't come back. It's hard enough getting Alex to school on time as it is without coping with a miniature whirlwind on four legs. *And* he's chewed my best shoes!'

'Well, he's just a puppy,' said Kate. 'That's what puppies do. You'll have to be careful to keep things out of his reach.'

'That's not a puppy, that's a fully grown dog and uncontrollable with it!'

'Nonsense,' she said briskly, and Derek squirmed with pleasure as she kissed the top of his head. 'You just need a bit of training, don't you? We'll have you sitting and staying in no time.'

Finn snorted. 'You take him, then, and while you're at it, train him to do something useful like make breakfast or tidy the kitchen.' He sighed as he took off his coat. 'God, what a morning! It's bad enough Alison being away without losing Rosa as well.'

'When is she coming back?' asked Kate, putting the dog back on the ground and trying not to feel hurt at the knowledge that he was missing Alison.

'Not soon enough!' Finn picked up the letters Kate had opened for him and began to flick through them. 'I'm not the most domesticated of men, and there's only so much take-away food that you can stomach. But Rosa's mother is still in hospital and she doesn't know how long she's going to be away.'

'Couldn't you get someone to help temporarily?'

'It's a bit difficult not knowing how long it would be for. Besides, Alex hates change. She doesn't like having a housekeeper at all and would rather it was just the two of us. She tolerates Rosa, but that's about as far as it goes.'

'I can see it's difficult,' said Kate, and Finn frowned as if recollecting too late that he was confiding his personal concerns.

'Yes, well, I'd better get on,' he said abruptly. 'Any messages?'

'Mr Osborne's PA rang. Could you call him back?'

'What does he want?'

Kate consulted her notebook. 'I gather he wants you to go and see him this afternoon. There are some points he wants to clarify before they make their final decision. What's the problem?' she asked as Finn cursed under his breath.

'I'll have to go. We can't afford to lose that contract, but I promised Alex I'd pick her up from school today as it's Friday. She wants everyone to see the dog.'

He stuck his hands in his pockets and frowned worriedly at the floor. 'She's always been a very solitary child—inevitable I suppose—but I hoped she'd make more friends at this new school. This morning's the first time she's shown any interest in what the other children thought,' he went on reluctantly. 'I'm afraid that if she's told everyone about the dog and he doesn't appear they'll think she's been making it up.'

'Why don't I go and meet her with Derek?' Kate offered, and his head jerked up to stare at her.

'You'd do that?'

Kate couldn't quite meet his eyes. She wasn't quite sure what had prompted her impulsive offer herself. It couldn't be wanting to ease the lines of strain around his mouth or the worry from his voice…could it?

'I wouldn't mind,' she said. 'It's partly my fault anyway. If I hadn't landed you with a dog, you wouldn't be in this situation.'

Finn hesitated. 'I might not get back until after seven if Osborne's in a nit-picking mood.'

'That's all right.' She busied herself sorting the papers on her desk into neat piles. 'I'll stay with Alex until you get home.'

'Are you sure? It's Friday night. Haven't you got anything planned?'

'Nothing special,' said Kate, 'and anyway, I can always go out later.'

'No heavy date with a financial analyst then?'

'What? Oh.' Colour crept into her cheeks as she remembered the elaborate story she had made up to impress him. 'No, that's the advantage of a fantasy man,' she said, putting up her chin. 'He fits in with all your other arrangements. He's the perfect man, really.'

'I see.' A disconcerting gleam lit Finn's grey eyes. 'Well, if you're sure you don't mind, I'd really appreciate it if you could go and meet Alex. I'll give you a note for the school and arrange for a car to take you there and then on home.'

Why was she doing this? Kate wondered as she sat with Derek in the back of the limousine Finn had booked. She had been so determined to stay cool and professional, too. Bella would say that she was getting involved, but she wasn't really. She was just helping out in a crisis. She'd do the same for anyone.

It was nothing whatsoever to do with the warm glow inside her when she remembered the almost-smile in Finn's eyes and the approval in his voice.

Because that wouldn't be at all professional, would it?

Standing at the school gates with all the other mothers and nannies was an odd experience. Kate could feel their curious sidelong glances at the impostor. She was sure they were all wondering what on earth she was doing there. What would it be like to be one of them, a bona fide mother instead of a pretend one? To be waiting for your own children, to take them home to the warmth and security of a loving home?

Kate had never allowed herself to think about having children too much. Even in the depths of her obsession with Seb she had known that he would be aghast at the very idea of children. Seb needed the world to revolve around him, and he wouldn't want to share the attention with anyone else, least of all a baby who wouldn't blend in with his décor. He was much too fickle and unreliable to make a good father anyway, unlike Finn.

Just for instance.

When the children started pouring out into the playground, Kate wrenched her mind away from the thought of Finn as a father and craned her neck to find Alex. She spotted her at last, searching the crowd in her turn for her father. Kate saw the moment when it dawned on her that he wasn't there, and sullenness masked the bitterness of her disappointment.

Pushing forward through the press of mothers and pushchairs with Derek, she waved to get her attention. 'Alex!' she called.

The terrible withdrawn look was wiped from Alex's face as she caught sight of Kate with the dog. It lit up instead and she rushed towards them.

'Dad's really sorry he couldn't come,' said Kate quickly, 'but he sent Derek instead. You don't mind, do you?'

'Not if Derek's here,' said Alex, crouching down so that the little dog could put his paws on her knees and greet her properly.

There was soon a circle of curious children staring at Derek. 'He's my dog,' said Alex nonchalantly, and Kate approved the careless way she dealt with the attention, as if it didn't matter to her whether anyone envied her or not.

Derek played his part brilliantly, greeting every child with enthusiasm and generally be-having in such an endearing way that none of them could resist asking Alex if they could pet him. He was clearly winning her lots of kudos in the playground, and her cheeks were pink with satisfaction when she finally left, holding tightly onto Derek's lead and waving a casual farewell.

The office was so modern and streamlined that Kate had somehow expected Finn to live somewhere similar, but it turned out to be a substantial Victorian house close to Wimbledon Common, with a large, safe gar-den. Ideal for a dog, in fact.

Inside, the house had evidently been deco-rated professionally, but it had a sterile, un-lived-in air that Kate thought was rather sad. It was a house and not a home, and she wondered whether it had been that way since Isabel had died.

Alex led the way to a big kitchen with French windows opening onto the garden. 'I wanted Derek to sleep in my room, but Dad said he had to stay here,' she told Kate, pointing out the basket and bowls set out in the corner.

'He's probably better off in the kitchen,' said Kate tactfully. That must have been another battle of wills. No wonder Finn had looked harassed this morning!

She looked around the kitchen while Alex had a drink and then, remembering what he had said about being sick of take-away food, suggested that they walk Derek along to the shops and buy something to cook for supper.

'You can cook?' Alex looked at her strangely.

'Well, nothing very impressive, but I can knock up the basics. What do you like to eat?'

Alex was fascinated by the fact that Kate knew how to make her favourite meal, macaroni cheese. 'Rosa doesn't make it, I don't think they have it where she comes from,' she said. 'Can you make puddings too?'

'Yes, some. Why, do you want a pudding as well?'

'Dad likes puddings, but Rosa's not very good at them either.'

Kate liked the idea of Finn having a weakness, even if it was only a sweet tooth. 'Do you think he'd like a chocolate pudding?' she asked Alex.

'Oh, yes, he loves chocolate.'

Better and better.

'Well, let's see what we can do.'

When Finn came home, he found his daughter, his temporary secretary and the dog in the kitchen. Unnoticed by any of them, he hesitated in the doorway, taking in the scene. Normally Alex retreated to her room, but today she was sitting happily at the kitchen table, the dog panting at her feet, helping Kate cook. There was flour everywhere and the sink was piled with dirty bowls and cooking implements. Alex's face was smudged with chocolate, and Kate's was not much better.

It struck Finn that he had never seen the kitchen look messier or more welcoming.

Kate was wearing Rosa's apron. She looked warm and dishevelled, her cheeks pink and her brown curls tumbled. As Finn watched, she lifted a hand to push her hair back from her face, leaving a streak of flour on her forehead.

'Not much of a guard dog, is he?' Finn's sarcasm disguised the sudden dryness in his throat.

At the sound of his voice, Kate started and Derek leapt belatedly to his feet, barking and wagging his tail so furiously that it would have taken a much harder heart than Finn's not to feel gratified at the warmth of his welcome.

'He's pleased to see you,' Alex told him as he bent to kiss his daughter.

Kate bent her head over the bowl into which she was sifting flour and tried to get her breathing back to normal. The sudden sight of Finn in the doorway had sent her heart lurching into her throat, where it lodged, jerking madly.

Shock at seeing him so unexpectedly, Kate told herself, in which case she wished her heart would just calm down. There was nothing to get excited about. It was just Finn, Finn with his cool eyes and his stern mouth and dark, austere presence. Nothing to make her senses fizz, or the breath evaporate from her lungs. And absolutely no reason to suddenly feel so ridiculously, embarrassingly shy.

'Hello,' she croaked in return to his greeting and carried on sifting with a kind of desperation.

Under her lashes, she could see Finn taking off his jacket and wrenching at his tie to loosen it. 'Something smells good,' he said.

'Kate's made macaroni cheese.' Alex tugged at his sleeve excitedly. 'And I have to have some salad, but then there's a chocolate pudding. We made it especially for you.'

Finn glanced at Kate, who blushed hotly and made a big deal of banging the sieve against the edge of the bowl. 'Alex said you liked chocolate.'

'I do.'

'I hope you don't mind me taking over your kitchen like this,' said Kate awkwardly. 'I thought I might as well make supper for you since I was here.'

'Mind?' echoed Finn. 'I'm very grateful!'

He seemed less dour and formidable than usual, as if the rigidity had gone from his jaw and his spine. It was only natural, Kate thought. He was at home, so it wasn't surprising if he was more relaxed than at the office.

But it was more disturbing, too. She wasn't sure how to deal with Finn when he was being approachable like this, and it made her nervous in a way that his brusqueness didn't any more.

'I won't be long,' she said, uncertain as to what she ought to do now, 'and I'll tidy up before I go.'

'But you'll stay and eat with us, won't you?' said Finn, and Alex added her voice as well.

'Oh, yes, you must stay!'

He might be just being polite. Kate twisted the sieve between her hands. Part of her longed to stay, and the other part was apprehensive. She felt very odd, all jittery and jumpy and it was something to do with the way Finn was standing there, looking at her.

Don't do it. Wasn't that what Bella had said?

'Well, I—'

'You said you didn't have anything special on tonight,' Finn reminded her.

'No, but—'

'I'll get a taxi to take you home later,' he promised. And then, almost as if the words were forced out of him, 'Please stay.'

What could she say? 'All right,' said Kate. 'Thanks.'

At which point Finn really threw her by smiling. A real smile. At her. 'I'm the one who should be thanking you,' he said.

Kate's hands were shaking as he went to change. She had imagined what he would look like when he smiled often enough, but she was still unprepared for how it transformed his face, illuminating those piercing grey eyes and softening the hard mouth. It had only been a brief smile, enough to glimpse the whiteness of his teeth and the way it creased his cheek and the edges of his eyes, but hardly enough to justify the sudden weakness at her knees or the bump and thump of her heart which had already been working overtime ever since he walked into the kitchen.

Guiltily, Kate faced the fact. She was doing exactly what Bella had warned her against. She had felt sorry for Finn since learning his tragic story, and now she was fancying herself attracted to him.

Which was just silly. She had had enough of falling for unobtainable men, and they didn't come more unobtainable than Finn. Not only was he utterly committed to the memory of his dead wife, but he was her boss. Getting involved when she had to see him every day at the office was a bad idea.

A *very* bad idea given that Alison would be coming back soon, and then where would she be? She was supposed to be out there meeting someone with whom she could have some fun, Kate reminded herself, not stuck in a

Wimbledon kitchen with an apron on, all twitchy and flustered because Finn had smiled at her.

She was just going to have to pull herself together. She had helped him out today, but that was as far as it was going to go. She would have supper, Kate decided, and then she would leave and she wouldn't even *think* about getting any closer.

CHAPTER FIVE

'THIS is a nice room.'

Alex had gone to bed and Finn had suggested to Kate that they had coffee in the sitting room. He had pulled the heavy red curtains across the window to shut out the cold, dark night, and had put on a lamp in the corner. Now he bent to switch on the fire. It was gas, but the appearance of real flames was very effective.

A bit *too* effective, Kate thought. The flickering light made the room dark and intimate, and now she was even more nervous about being alone with him. It hadn't been too bad while Alex was there, but now there was only Derek as chaperon and, in spite of all her efforts to keep up a flow of bright conversation, a tension was seeping back into the atmosphere.

It was Finn's fault, she had decided. He looked different tonight. It was the first time she had seen him out of a suit. He'd changed before supper and, in casual trousers and a

114

warm shirt, he seemed younger, less austere, and Kate was disturbingly aware of him.

She tried not to look at him as he straightened from the fire and sat down at the other end of the sofa, which was when she was forced to make her inane comment about the room instead.

Finn glanced round as if he had never seen it before. 'I don't use this room very much,' he said. 'It's too big. I rattle around in it when I'm on my own. I usually sit in my study.'

Kate thought of this beautiful room sitting empty while Finn retreated to his study every night. 'It must get lonely sometimes,' she said, and felt Finn's eyes flicker to her face and then away.

'I'm used to it now,' he said.

Kate swirled the wine around the bottom of her glass. 'Do you miss her all the time?' she asked, emboldened by the darkness and the firelight.

'Isabel?' Finn sighed and stared into the flames. 'It was hell at first, but now...it comes and goes. Sometimes I think I've accepted that she's gone and others I miss her so much it's like a physical pain. I look at Alex and I get angry that she didn't get the chance to see her daughter growing up.'

'I'm sorry,' said Kate quietly, not knowing what else she could say.

Finn looked across at her again, his face unreadable in the dim light. 'You know what happened?'

'Someone at work told me it was a car accident.'

He nodded. 'She was in a coma for a week. I couldn't do anything, I could only sit there and hold her hand and tell her how much I loved her.' He turned back to the fire. 'The doctors said she couldn't hear me.'

Kate's throat ached for him. 'Maybe she could feel you.'

'That's what I told myself. I promised her that I would look after Alex, that I'd do on my own, for both of us, but I'm beginning to wonder if I can keep that promise.'

Draining the last of his wine, Finn leant forward to put the glass on the coffee-table in front of them. 'It's hard being a single parent. The worst bit is not having anyone to share your worries with. Alex can be difficult sometimes, and that's when I miss Isabel most. She was so calm and gentle. She would know how to handle her.'

'But Alex seems very happy,' said Kate, thinking of the way the little girl had chattered through supper.

'Thanks to you.'

Kate's jaw dropped. 'To me?'

'She's happier now than I've seen her for a very long time, and it's because of that mutt you gave us.' He stirred Derek with his foot where he lay under the coffee-table, and ecstatic at the least bit of attention, the dog rolled over onto his back with a sigh of contentment.

'Alex doesn't make friends easily,' Finn went on. 'She's very reserved for a child. I worry that she's too possessive of me, too.'

'I suppose that's inevitable when it's just the two of you,' said Kate.

'Perhaps.' He leant forward, resting his elbows on his knees, and the firelight cast flickering shadows across his face, highlighting then concealing the lines of strain. 'She resents the fact that we have to have a housekeeper, and doesn't understand why it can't just be the two of us.

'I've thought about selling the company and staying at home,' he admitted, 'but what would happen to everyone who's worked for me so loyally, and what would I do with myself? Alex is at school all day. There's only so much cooking and cleaning I can do, and I'd still have to make a living somehow.'

Finn hunched his shoulders. He had obviously been over his options again and again. 'The other alternative, of course, is to marry again,' he said. 'Alex is growing up. She's going to need a woman around even more, but it doesn't seem fair to ask someone to marry me just to be a stepmother...'

He trailed off with a hopeless gesture. He sounded so tired that Kate had a terrifying impulse to put her arms around him, to draw his head down onto her breast and tell him that everything would be all right, that she was there.

Not the best way to go about not getting involved.

Swallowing hard, she stared at the fire instead. 'Is that why you came to dinner with Gib and Phoebe? Looking for a suitable stepmother?'

'Partly,' said Finn. 'I'd talked myself into making an effort to go out and meet more people. I thought maybe if I actually met someone, things might change somehow, but...'

'But you just met me,' Kate finished for him.

'Yes,' said Finn after a moment. 'I met you.'

There was a silence. To Kate it seemed to last for ever, fraught with unspoken implications. That she wasn't the kind of stepmother he was looking for, that she hadn't changed anything for him. Or that she might have done if she hadn't turned out to be working for him?

Or if she hadn't been determined not to get involved, of course.

It was Finn who broke the silence. 'What were *you* doing there?'

'Phoebe's one of my best friends.'

'Did you know I was going to be there?'

'Yes. I didn't know it was *you* of course,' Kate added hurriedly, 'but I knew that they'd invited someone for me to meet.'

Finn looked at her curiously. 'I don't understand it.'

'What do you mean?'

'You're a pretty girl,' he said. 'You must know that. You're lively, intelligent—when you want to be, anyway—and you've obviously got lots of friends. I'd have thought men would be queuing up to take you out. Why would a girl like you need her friends to fix her up on a blind date?'

Kate shrugged. 'It's not as easy as you think, especially when you get past thirty. All the nice men are settled in relationships, usually with your friends, and you end up making a fool of yourself over the ones that are available.' A tinge of bitterness crept into her voice. 'That's what seems to happen to me, anyway.'

'Not Will the financial analyst?'

'No.' Kate half smiled. She might as well admit it. 'Will exists all right, but he's Bella's boyfriend, not mine. I just borrowed him for my little fantasy to try and impress you. Not that it worked.'

'I don't know,' said Finn. 'You had me convinced for a while.'

Without thinking, Kate had made herself more comfortable, putting her feet up onto the coffee-table and leaning back into the cushions so that she could rest her head against the back of the sofa. Finn's eyes rested on her face.

'So if it wasn't Will, who was it?'

'His name's Seb.' Kate looked up at the ceiling, remembering. 'I was mad about him. He was one of the junior executives where I used to work, and I used to fantasise about him from afar. He was so good-looking and charming and he had a terrible reputation—but of course, that was part of his appeal,' she said ironically. 'When he noticed me amongst all the other girls there, I couldn't believe my luck.'

She sighed a little. 'Phoebe and Bella never liked him, but I was in thrall to him. It's hard to explain now. He had this kind of sexual charisma. I couldn't think properly when I was with him.

'I told them they didn't understand him the way I did. I persuaded myself that his selfishness was a result of the way he'd been brought up and that there was a little lost boy inside him. I thought that all he needed was the love of a good woman, and that I'd be the one to change him, you know the sort of thing.' She laughed but there was an undercurrent of bitterness to it. 'I was such a fool.'

'We all make mistakes,' said Finn neutrally.

'Most people learn from theirs. I didn't.' Kate leant forward to pick up her coffee. 'We had what magazines call a ''destructive relationship''. I humiliated myself for months. I'd go out of my way just to bump into him, and wait desperately for him to call. I got obsessed with checking the phone and my email, and Seb knew it. He'd say that he would contact me, then he'd ignore my existence, until I'd just given up hope.

'He always timed it perfectly. He'd ring or drop round out of the blue, and I'd be so pleased to see him that I didn't realise until too late that he was only there because he wanted something. He wanted to borrow some money or get his washing done.'

Kate caught Finn's look. 'Oh, yes,' she said with a rueful smile. 'I'd wash and iron and cook and clean for him. I cringe when I think about it now, but at the time it seemed the only way I could keep him.'

She must sound completely pathetic. Finn would probably despise such spineless behaviour, but it was hard to tell from his expression what he was thinking.

'What made you change your mind about him?' was all he asked.

'I went up to his office one evening,' Kate told him. 'I'd found an excuse to work late as usual, knowing that he'd be there, and I found him shouting at one of the cleaners. I don't even know what she was supposed to have done, but the poor woman was terrified. English obviously wasn't her first language, and I just hoped that she couldn't understand half the things he was calling her.

'It was horrible,' she said with a shudder at the memory. 'I couldn't believe how unpleasant he was! When I told him he couldn't talk to people like, he turned on me, and we had a huge argument. I ended up saying that I was going to report him for verbal abuse.'

'And what did Seb say to that?'

'He told me not to bother, because *he* was going to report *me* for harassment.'

'And who do you think they're going to believe?' Seb had sneered. 'A not very efficient secretary or a rising executive?'

'That's exactly what he did,' Kate finished. 'And I lost my job.'

Finn was looking grim. 'Couldn't you fight it?'

'The trouble was that everyone knew I was mad about him, and the way I'd made excuses to see him made it easy for him to make everyone believe that I was practically stalking him. Of course he didn't tell anyone about the times he showed up on *my* doorstep.'

'Is that why you had to leave your job?' Finn sounded even grimmer now.

'Yes. Oh, I wasn't sacked. Nothing as crude as that. It was merely suggested that I might be happier elsewhere, and that if I stayed my position might become ''untenable''.' Kate hooked her fingers in the air to add extra emphasis to the pomposity of the phrases they had used.

Seb had been promoted. She didn't tell Finn that.

'You should have appealed,' he said, frowning.

She shrugged. 'By that stage I didn't want to work there any longer anyway. It was ironic, really. After all those months desperate to catch a glimpse of Seb, the moment I didn't want to see him any more, he seemed to be around the whole time. I was glad to leave.

'The only trouble was that they gave me a really grudging reference, which meant I couldn't get another job,' she went on. 'Joining the temp agency was my only option in the end, and working for you is my first job with them.' No harm in reassuring Finn that she hadn't forgotten that their relationship was strictly professional.

She smiled brightly at him. 'That's why I have to try and make a good impression and stick with you until Alison gets back.'

It was true. If Finn gave her a rotten report, she might find herself off the agency's list, but Kate didn't think there was any need to labour the point.

'Is that what you're doing now?' he said, putting his coffee-mug very deliberately back onto the coffee table.

'Now?' she echoed blankly.

'Picking Alex up from school, making supper, all of this.' There was a harsh note in his voice, almost as if he was disappointed.

'No,' said Kate. 'I didn't even think about it. Besides, the ability to make macaroni cheese isn't the kind of thing employers look for in a reference. I was just hoping you'd notice that I was being more punctual and efficient.'

'I see,' was all Finn said, but he sounded less hard.

'It's all part of my new attitude,' Kate went on to make sure he understood that she was in absolutely no danger of misinterpreting that they were alone in the dark and firelight.

'I've decided to sharpen up my act all round. Seb taught me a valuable lesson—two, in fact. From now on I'm going to keep my personal life quite separate from work, and I'm not going to get too serious about anyone. I'm going to take any opportunity to meet new people, even if it means going on a blind date. So when Phoebe rang and said they had invited someone to meet me, I thought ''why not''? I wasn't interested in finding a deep and meaningful relationship,' she told him. 'I just wanted some fun.'

'But you just met me,' Finn quoted Kate's words back to her.

Something in his voice made Kate turn her head. He was watching her from the other end of the sofa, his expression unreadable, but his eyes trapped hers without warning, stopping the breath in her throat and holding her mouse-still, skewered by the directness of his gaze. Kate wasn't sure how long they sat there with the air evaporating around them, and the silence stretching unbearably, broken only by the faint hiss and splutter of the gas fire and the booming roar of her pulse in her ear, but when Finn looked away it was like being released from a pinion-hold.

Now all she had to do was remember what they had been talking about before she turned her head.

Ah, yes. Impressing on him that she was just out to have a good time and not in the market for marriage or anything remotely serious. So he needn't panic.

'Yes, it was a bit of a shock.' She forced a smile. 'It's not much fun to find yourself on a blind date with your boss.'

'No,' said Finn, looking into the fire. 'I imagine not.'

*   *   *

It was all very well convincing Finn that she just wanted to have a good time, but Kate found it harder to live up to in practice. There was no problem about going out. Bella was relentlessly social, and Kate could always tag along with her. But somehow going out wasn't quite as much fun as it had used to be.

Kate was exasperated to find herself in the middle of a party, fretting about how Finn and Alex were managing with the housekeeper still away. It wasn't her problem, she reminded herself endlessly. She was supposed to be having fun and being cool, and worrying about grieving widowers and motherless children wasn't part of the plan.

Sitting in a bar with a City type baying at her about his bonuses and his flash car, or pretending to study the menu in a crowded restaurant, Kate would find her mind wandering to the house in Wimbledon. She thought about Alex and the little dog, but mostly she thought about Finn, sitting at the other end of the sofa in the firelight. She thought about the way his smile illuminated the severe face, about the line of that stern mouth and, whenever she did, which was too often for comfort, something twisted and churned inside her.

It was even worse in the office, though. She was jittery and on edge in the same room as Finn, and if he came anywhere near her she would suddenly become clumsy, spilling her coffee or dropping papers, and colouring painfully when he looked at her in surprise.

Only three weeks until Alison was due back. Kate wasn't sure whether she longed for an end to the daily embarrassment of making a complete fool of herself, or dreaded it. Sometimes she tried to imagine working for someone else, in a different office, but she just couldn't do it. No dog to walk every lunch time. No willing her nerves not to jump whenever Finn walked into the room.

No Finn.

Ever since that evening when she had picked Alex up from school the atmosphere between them had been one of careful constraint. Finn was gruff but polite, and Kate found herself wishing more than once that he would go back to shouting at her and being grumpy and generally disagreeable. Things had been easier then.

Somehow Kate struggled through to the Friday, but by that afternoon she was in no fit state to deal with the long and complicated list of instructions Finn decided to give her. Sitting across the desk from him, she was supposed to be taking notes, but she kept getting diverted by the sight of his hands as he moved papers around, or letting her eyes rest on his mouth while he searched for a particular bit of information, and then when he looked up again, his eyes would be so piercing that she instantly lost track of what she was supposed to be doing.

'Are you all right?' Finn asked at last, after she had had to ask him to repeat himself for the sixth time.

'I'm fine,' stammered Kate, colour rushing into her cheeks. Honestly, it was getting to the point where she couldn't talk to him without blushing like an idiot.

'It's just that you seem even vaguer than usual today.'

'No, I'm a bit tired that's all,' she said. 'I had a late night.' That was true enough, she had been out with Bella. 'We went out to a club, and you know what it's like when you're having good time,' she went on, spotting another opportunity to persuade Finn that, while she might be behaving like a love-struck schoolgirl, it was nothing whatsoever to do with him.

'You forget to look at your watch,' she told him, all ditzy brunette, the kind of girl who danced till the small hours and whose only aim in life was to have fun. The last kind of girl to waste her time even *thinking* about a man preoccupied with domestic problems.

'I'll take your word for it,' said Finn dryly.

He paused, shuffling papers unnecessarily. 'I told Alex that you had a very social life,' he said unexpectedly, 'but I promised her that I'd ask you anyway.'

'Ask me what?' said Kate, surprised into normality.

'She seems to regard you as an authority on dogs. God knows, you've got to know more than we do anyway! Anyway, she wanted to know if you'd come over and show her how to train Derek one afternoon this weekend. Apparently you told her that you would give her a few tips,' he went on almost accusingly, as if the invitation was her fault somehow.

She *had* promised Alex that she would show her how to train Derek, Kate remembered. That wasn't the problem. The problem was how much she wanted to go.

'I told her you'd be busy,' Finn said as she hesitated.

'No...no...I'm not busy,' said Kate, who had opened her mouth to take the let-out clause he offered and found herself saying something completely different instead.

'I mean, an afternoon would be fine,' she stumbled on, her mouth still operating contrary to strict orders from her brain which was telling her to do the sensible thing and not get any more involved than she was already. 'Perhaps we could go for a walk on one of the parks?'

'That's kind of you,' Finn said in such a stilted voice that Kate wondered if he had wanted her to refuse. 'Alex will be pleased.'

What about you? she wanted to ask him. Will you be pleased?

'Would Sunday afternoon suit you?' he was saying, still repressively polite.

'Sunday would be fine.'

'We'll come and pick you up in the car. About two o'clock?'

In spite of giving herself a good talking to on the way home, and reminding herself of all the reasons why she didn't want to get involved with Finn or his daughter or his dog, Kate was appalled at how much she looked forward to Sunday afternoon. Saturday night, another wild session orchestrated by Bella, was just an endurance test, and she left as early as she decently could, hoping that Bella wouldn't notice her lack of enthusiasm.

No such luck. 'What is up with you at the moment?' Bella accused her when she finally emerged, yawning and tousled, on Sunday morning.

'Nothing,' said Kate brightly.

'I lined up Will's friend specially for you, and you blew him off. I thought Toby would be just your type.'

'He was OK.' Kate fidgeted around the kitchen, putting jars and packets away, and wiping down the work surface with a cloth.

Bella looked at her in deep suspicion. 'And why are you tidying the kitchen suddenly?'

'No reason,' said Kate. 'It's just a mess.'

'It's always a mess and it never bothered you before. Who's coming round?'

'Finn and his daughter might come later.' Kate tried to sound casual, but she should have known better than to try and fool Bella.

'Finn as in the boss you hated and then felt sorry for? The one you had no intention of getting involved with?'

'Yes,' she had to admit.

'Explain to me how having him round to your house on a Sunday afternoon is not being involved?'

'If you must know, it's a date with his daughter. We're going to take the dog for a walk, and Finn's just going to drive us from A to B.'

'Right,' said Bella, obviously not believing a word.

'It's true. I'm only going because I feel a bit responsible for the dog.'

Bella filled the kettle at the sink. 'So what will I tell Toby if he rings and wants to see you again?'

'Absolutely,' said Kate firmly. 'I'm into fun, fun, fun.'

'That'll be why you're getting ready for a *walk* about four hours early! What are you going to wear?'

Oh, God, good point. What *was* she going to wear? Back in her bedroom, Kate rummaged through her clothes. She really must hang some of those skirts up some time.

It was all too difficult. She didn't want to look a mess, but she didn't want to look as if she was trying too hard either. Her jeans were a bit tight, but she squeezed into them and pulled on a red jumper which was one of her favourites. Not that Finn was likely to see it under her jacket, of course.

Unless she offered them some tea? And scones might be nice after a cold walk.

Kate galloped back down to the kitchen and began burrowing through the cupboards for flour and cream of tartar.

'Do you know if we've got any bicarb of soda?'

Bella looked up from the gossip pages in the Sunday paper. 'What do you want that for?'

'I thought I might make some scones,' said Kate carelessly.

'Scones?' Bella shook her head. 'You have got it bad!' and then when Kate swung round to protest, 'try the cupboard above the toaster.'

Kate fidgeted around the kitchen for the rest of the morning, driving Bella mad by trying to tidy up around her.

'I wish this Finn would just come and put you out of your misery,' Bella grumbled as she gathered up the paper and her coffee and retreated to the sitting room.

By the time the doorbell rang, Kate had worked herself up to a pitch of nerves she couldn't remember since her very first date. Pulling down her jumper, she ran her fingers through her curls and took a deep breath before opening the door.

Finn was standing behind Alex, and Kate's heart gave a great lurch when she saw him. She looked quickly away at Alex, who greeted her with an unselfconscious hug. In similar circumstances Kate would think nothing of kissing a visitor like Finn on the cheek, but the thought of touching him, however briefly, seemed fraught with difficulty, and in the end she contented herself with smiling stiffly.

'Hello.'

Alex sat in the back seat with an overexcited Derek. She was in a chatty mood, so all Kate had to do was nod and smile and put in the occasional comment, which was just as well as she was having trouble concentrating with Finn's hand moving competently on the gears so close to her knee.

It was a relief to get out of the car and concentrate on Alex and the dog. She showed her how to offer little treats when Derek did as he was told, and before long he was sitting and waiting until he was called before he came lolloping towards her.

Alex was delighted. 'He's clever, isn't he, Dad?'

'Clever enough to know what it takes to get some food,' said Finn, who had been watching them with a resigned expression.

Afterwards they walked around the park. It was a cold, blustery day and the wind blew Kate's hair around her face. Alex ran ahead with Derek, while Kate tried not to be too conscious of Finn striding beside her, his head down, his hands thrust into the pockets of his jacket, his dark hair ruffled by the breeze.

Every now and then Alex would come galloping back, her cheeks pink and her eyes shining behind her glasses. 'I wish we could do this every weekend!'

'You never liked walking before,' said Finn.

'It's different if you've got a dog. I'm so glad you came to work for Dad,' she told Kate fervently. 'Aren't you, Dad?'

Finn glanced at Kate, who was trying unsuccessfully to hold her hair back from her face. Her brown eyes were bright in the sharp light and the exercise had brought colour to her cheeks.

'She's certainly changed my life,' he said, and Kate smiled uncertainly, not sure how to take that. Was changing his life a good thing or a bad thing, or was he just joking?

In the end, she decided it would be safer just to ignore it. She asked about the housekeeper instead. 'Will Rosa be coming back soon?'

'We don't know. She's been very good about keeping in touch and she's obviously anxious not to lose the job, but her mother's still very ill and she just can't tell when she'll be able to leave her. In the meantime, Alex and I are managing as best we can.'

'It's great,' said Alex. 'It's much better without a housekeeper at all.'

'You won't think so when your Aunt Stella arrives,' Finn said. 'She'll be horrified that there's no one to look after you properly.'

'You look after me,' Alex said loyally, tucking her hand into his, and Kate saw the rueful twist of his smile.

'Stella will tell me I'm not enough, and she'll be right.'

'Who's Stella?' she asked.

'She's Dad's sister. She's so bossy!'

'She lives in Canada,' Finn said, more measured. 'She comes over here every year to make sure Alex and I are all right.'

He hesitated. 'She's got a good heart, but she can be a bit…domineering.'

'Bossy,' said Alex.

'Overbearing,' Finn overruled her and turned back to Kate, ignoring the way his daughter muttered an insistent 'Bossy!' under her breath. 'Stella decided a couple of years ago that Alex needed a stepmother, and now whenever she's over she lines up a string of what she thinks are suitable women for me to meet.'

'They're always awful too,' Alex put in. 'Aren't they, Dad?'

'Let's just say that Stella has different ideas from us about the kind of stepmother Alex needs,' said Finn. 'I'm fond of her, and I know she means well, but I wish she'd just let me organise my life my own way.'

Kate was intrigued. 'I can't imagine you being bossed about by anybody,' she confessed.

'You don't know my sister! It's a pity, because now Alex and I dread her visits.'

'You know what we should do, Dad?' said Alex, skipping along beside them.

'What?'

'We should pretend that you've already got a girlfriend, then Aunt Stella wouldn't be able to say anything.'

'I don't think Stella is that easy to fool,' said Finn wryly. 'She'd insist on meeting any girlfriend, and we'd look a bit stupid if we couldn't produce one, wouldn't we?'

'Maybe we could ask Kate to pretend,' suggested Alex.

'Pretend what?'

'Pretend to be your girlfriend.' Alex bounced up and down as she realised the full potential of her idea. 'You could say that you were going to get married. That would shut Aunt Stella up!'

There was an uncomfortable silence. Kate's heart had lurched oddly at Alex's suggestion, but she knew that she had to treat it as a joke, so she forced a laugh to show that she wouldn't even *think* of taking the suggestion seriously.

'I don't think that's a very good idea,' said Finn after a moment.

'Why not? Kate wouldn't mind, would you, Kate?'

Kate made a noncommittal noise, which seemed the only option.

'It would be fun,' Alex went on. 'Imagine Aunt Stella's face when she comes in all ready to bully you into getting married and you told her that you'd found someone without her interfering! I think it would be great.'

'That's enough, Alex,' her father said sharply.

'But why not?' Alex insisted. 'We could have a nice time instead of spending our whole time trying to avoid those women Aunt Stella insists on inviting round.'

'I *said*, that's enough!'

Alex subsided, muttering sullenly, before working off her bad mood by throwing sticks for Derek.

'I'm sorry about that,' said Finn when she had run off. 'She gets a bit carried away.'

'That's all right.' There was another awkward pause. 'Is your sister really that bad?' Kate asked after a moment.

'Worse,' he sighed. 'I know it's just because she worries about Alex, and I know she's right, but she's a very...forceful personality.'

'Really?' Kate was unable to resist murmuring. 'Fancy you being related!'

Finn shot her a sharp look but evidently decided to ignore her ironic interruption. 'She and Alex have clashed ever since Alex realised what Stella was trying to do. The thing about Stella is that she hasn't got a lot of tact and she thinks she can bully people into doing what she thinks is the right thing. She's always been the same.'

Kate tried to imagine a female version of Finn, and quailed at the thought. Stella sounded very scary.

'Can't you just tell her that you and Alex are happy with the way things are?'

'Believe me, I've tried,' said Finn. 'The thing is, I owe her a lot. It was Stella who kept things together when Isabel died. I don't know what I'd have done without her. She's a good person to have around in a crisis. She lives in Canada and has her own family, but she came straight over and looked after Alex—and me—until I could cope.

'I've told her that I can see that she's got a point, and I'll think about getting married again, but Stella thinks that unless she nags and bullies and introduces endless divorcees I'll never get round to it. And the truth is that it's hard to face up to trying to meet women when Alex is so against the idea, so in a way she's right. I just wish she wouldn't go on about it so much.'

CHAPTER SIX

'IT'S hard when people care about you,' said Kate. Her collar was turned up against the wind, and her hands were deep in her pockets to stop them wandering over towards Finn of their own accord.

'When I was going out with Seb, Bella and Phoebe used to go on and on about how bad he was for me. Deep down, I knew they were right, but it didn't make it any easier somehow. I couldn't be cross with them because I knew it was only because they loved me and wanted me to be happy, but sometimes,' she admitted, 'I wished they would just shut up and leave me alone.'

Their pace had slowed without either of them realising it, and now Finn stopped and looked down at Kate, a curious expression in his flinty grey eyes. 'Yes, that's just what I feel about Stella,' he said.

Clouds were scudding across the sky in the wind, and for a moment the sun broke through the greyness like a biblical picture. To Kate it was as if the two of them were standing alone in an intense beam of light that held them motionless, breathless, isolated from everyone else in the park. She was intensely aware of her heart beating, and the blood pulsing through her veins, of the flecking of silvery light in Finn's cool grey eyes and the dark ring around his pupils.

Then the clouds shut out the sun again, like someone switching off a light, and Alex was running back, calling to Derek, and Finn looked away. Kate felt oddly shaken and disorientated. Her heart was beating in her throat and there was a constricted feeling in her chest, so that she had to concentrate to breathe.

Finn cleared his throat and made a big deal of looking at his watch. 'Maybe we should think about going back.'

Kate was very glad of Alex's chatter as they drove back to Tooting. She felt very strange. Her body was thumping and there was a disturbing quiver deep inside her that made her excruciatingly aware of Finn, of his hand shifting gear, of his eyes flicking to the mirror, of the turn of his head.

She really *must* pull herself together! All he had done was meet her eyes for a few seconds, and for all she knew he was thinking about something else entirely. Anyone would think he had pulled her down on the grass and made mad, passionate love the way she was carrying on!

What had made her think of *that*? The image was so clear that Kate caught her breath and she had to stare desperately out of the side window, trying to force the picture of what it might be like if Finn did pull her towards him, did kiss her, did let his hands slide over her body, out of her mind. But it was as if the thought was lodged there now, so real and so vivid that Kate was terrified it was emblazoned across her face.

Finn found a parking space right in front of the house, and switched off the engine. 'Would you like to come in and have some tea?' Kate heard herself asking into the sudden silence. Her voice came out all funny, thin and high, as if she was really nervous or something. 'I've got some scones.'

'Proper tea!' said Alex approvingly. 'Can Derek come?'

'Of course.'

In fact, Derek got an extremely frosty reception from Kate's cat, who had been curled up comfortably on the sofa and was outraged to find himself nudged by a cold, wet nose attached to a tail wagged in tentative greeting.

Arching his back, he puffed out his fur and hissed, adding a swipe of his paw to reinforce the message.

'What's his name?' asked Alex as Derek squealed and backed off hastily.

'We just call him Cat,' said Kate. 'He was a stray like Derek, but he was practically wild when I brought him back. He used to bite our ankles and scratch and Phoebe refused to let me give him a name because she said I'd want to keep him then. But I could never find a home for him, so we just got used to calling him Cat.'

'He wouldn't have gone anyway,' said Bella who had been lying in one of the chairs painting her nails when they came in. 'Say what you like about that cat, he's not stupid and he knows he'd never find a sucker like Kate anywhere else!'

She smiled at Finn and Alex. 'If you want to be spoiled to death and never do anything in return, Kate's your gal! I'm sure all the stray animals in London have passed the word around about what a pushover she is, because they're always turning up on the doorstep, holding up a paw and looking needy.'

'Bella, I'm sure they don't want to hear all those stories,' said Kate with a meaningful glare at her friend. Once Bella got started, there was no stopping her.

'Yes we do!' Alex piped up, and Bella grinned.

'Of course they do,' she said with an unrepentant wink at her friend, and proceeded to regale Alex and Finn with her repertoire of stories, each one more exaggerated than the last and all illustrating Kate's ridiculously soft heart and/or capacity to get herself into an unholy muddle.

Bella was outrageous, but knew how to lay on the charm, and she could be very funny. Alex was giggling and even Finn's mouth twitched occasionally.

Mortified, Kate fumbled around making tea and heating up the scones. She could feel Finn's eyes on her every now and then. Probably wondering how such an idiot could ever have been taken on by the temp agency, she thought gloomily.

'I hope you realise she's making most of these stories up,' she said as she carried the tray over to the comfortable chairs where they were sitting.

'I am not!' Bella protested.

'Grossly exaggerating, then. I notice you never tell any stories which show me as intelligent and sophisticated!'

'There aren't any of those, Kate!'

'Very funny,' said Kate mirthlessly, but at least Bella was diverted by the scones.

'I could tell loads of stories about what a good cook you are,' she offered.

'We already know that,' said Finn, glancing at Kate, who immediately started blushing and stammering that she wasn't really, honestly, she just muddled her way through recipes like everyone else...

A story that showed her as sophisticated? Dream on, Kate, she thought, listening to herself with a sinking heart.

Bella looked from Finn to Kate, blue eyes suddenly speculative. Kate could practically see her deciding to unleash the full force of her considerable charm on Finn, and just hoped he was ready for it. Bella on top form was hard to resist, and Kate wondered if Finn guessed quite how thoroughly he was being interrogated. Judging by his responses, which were civil but not exactly revealing, she guessed that he had a good suspicion of it anyway, and she didn't know whether to be glad or sorry that he was apparently impervious to her friend.

'This is a nice kitchen,' Alex said when Finn started to make a move. 'I wish ours was more like this, Dad.'

Kate could see Finn looking around the clutter, the empty bottles waiting to be recycled, the magazines strewn everywhere, Bella's nail polishes, the lingerie drying haphazardly on the airer. He didn't actually wince, but he might as well have done.

'It takes a lot of work to keep a room as messy as this,' she told Alex solemnly. 'I'm not sure your father's up to it.'

She felt quite giddy when Finn laughed. He actually laughed at something she'd said! 'You've obviously had years of experience,' he said, oblivious to the way her heart was somersaulting around her chest at the whiteness of his teeth and the deep crease in his cheeks and the humour crinkling the edges of his eyes.

'I like to practise at the office, too,' she said a little breathlessly, and then he smiled again.

'I can tell,' he said.

Bella was finishing off the last scone when Kate came back from seeing them all to the car, her elation evaporated by the mundane nature of Finn's farewell. She had hugged Alex and patted Derek, but Finn made sure that things were firmly back on a neutral footing.

'See you tomorrow,' was all he had said.

Well, what had she expected? That he would be flinging his arms round her or drawing her close for a passionate kiss? It would take more than a laugh for Finn to forget that they had to go back to work.

Back to reality.

'Yes, see you tomorrow,' Kate echoed flatly.

'Not very forthcoming, is he?' mumbled Bella through a mouthful of scone.

Kate didn't pretend not to know who she meant. Drearily, she began gathering up the tea things. 'He's...private,' she said.

'He's that all right. I've never met anyone that hard to read.'

Kate was conscious of a twist of disappointment. More than a twist, if she was honest. A pang would describe it better. Or a knife turning in her gut.

She didn't want Bella to find Finn unreadable. Her friend was so much more perceptive than she was. She wanted her to confide that she had seen Finn watching Kate, perhaps, or that having talked to him it was obvious that he was in love with her. If there had been the slightest hint of anything like that, Bella would have spotted it.

But there hadn't been.

'It doesn't bother me,' she said, even managing a creditable shrug. 'As far as I'm concerned, he's just my boss, and only temporarily at that. I don't particularly want to know every last detail about his private life.'

The trouble was that Bella was just as perceptive about her as she was about everybody else. 'Sure,' she said, then she got up and put an arm round Kate's shoulders. 'Never mind,' she consoled her. 'There's always chocolate!'

'Finn McBride's office,' Kate answered the phone the following Tuesday.

'This is Alison, Finn's PA,' a cool voice told her.

'Oh…hello. How's your leg?'

'Much better, thank you. How have you been getting on?' There was a slight but distinct note of condescension in Alison's voice that made Kate bristle.

'Fine, I think,' she said, striving for equal coolness. 'Would you like to speak to Finn?'

'Please.' Alison sounded as if she disapproved of Kate calling him Finn instead of Mr

McBride. Perhaps you were supposed to be his PA for five years before you were allowed to use his Christian name.

'I'll put you through,' said Kate evenly.

Finn came out of his office a few minutes later. 'That was Alison,' he said unnecessarily.

'Oh,' said Kate, convinced that Alison's call would have reminded him of how efficient and reliable she was. Unlike her temporary replacement.

'The doctor has said that she can come back to work next Monday.'

'Next Monday?' Kate was unable to keep the dismay from her voice. She had been expecting to stay at least another couple of weeks. Monday's too soon, she wanted to shout.

Finn cleared his throat. 'I told her there was no need to come back before she was ready, but she says she's keen to get back to things.'

'I see.' What else could she say?

'I thought...you might be staying a bit longer,' he said.

There was an awkward pause, as if neither of them knew what to say next.

'Well,' said Kate eventually with an attempt at heartiness, 'that's good news.'

'Yes,' said Finn, not sounding entirely convinced.

'You'll have a bit more organisation in the office again.' She glanced at Derek who had trotted in beside Finn and now flung himself panting at her feet. 'No stray dogs, anyway.'

'No.'

'I'd better tidy my desk,' said Kate after another agonising pause. She looked at the piles of papers and files without enthusiasm. Three days wasn't long to sort some order out of the chaos.

She forced a bright smile. 'Shall I get Personnel to ring the agency and let them know?'

'What agency?' asked Finn, who was standing by the window with his hands in his pockets, staring down at the street.

'The temp agency. They might be able to find me another job for Monday.'

'Oh.' He turned. 'Right. Yes.' He looked at Kate, and then away, as if he wanted to say something but had thought better of it. 'Yes, you'd better do that.'

So that was it then. Just as well she hadn't got involved, thought Kate as she sat miserably on the bus that night. And she *wasn't* involved, whatever Bella might say. She had always known that there was no point in falling for Finn. She didn't want to spend her entire life being second-best to the beautiful, perfect, irreplaceable Isabel. That had been decided after intensive chocolate therapy on Sunday evening.

She wanted fun, fun, fun instead.

Somehow that had been easier to believe after the stiff vodka and tonic prescribed by Bella than it did now when she had to face up to the fact that after Friday she would never see Finn again.

The last three days were agony. Finn was taciturn and any conversation they did have was stilted in the extreme. By the time Friday came round, Kate almost began to be glad that she was leaving. At least she wouldn't have to endure this awful, constrained atmosphere any longer.

When Finn called her into his room, she braced herself for him to say something about her leaving. She had already decided how she was going to be: friendly but professional. He had to say something, surely, if only to sort out what to do about Derek, who had now become a familiar part of the office routine. Kate tripped over him at least six times a day.

She could hardly believe it when Finn merely asked her to tidy up a few matters before Alison came back. 'We want to try and leave things as clear for her as possible,' he said.

Right, they didn't want his precious Alison to have to do too much when she came back, did they? Kate was furious. OK, she might not be Alison, but she had been here six weeks, and she had worked really hard, not to mention walking his dog for him every lunchtime. It wouldn't kill him to say thank you.

'Is that it?' she asked him coldly as she got to her feet.

'There is just one thing,' said Finn almost reluctantly. His eyes rested on Kate, who was clutching her notebook to her chest and looking cross and ruffled. 'Sit down,' he added.

Kate sank resentfully back onto the edge of her chair and opened her notebook once more with martyred sigh. Pen poised, she looked at him. 'Yes?' she prompted him.

'You don't need to take notes,' he said with an edge of his old irritation. 'I was only going to ask if you'd got a job lined up for Monday.'

'Oh.' Kate lowered her pen. She had been trying not to think about Monday. 'No, not yet.'

'How would you feel about a change of career?' asked Finn carefully.

She stared at him. 'What?'

'You mentioned when we were at dinner with Gib and Phoebe that you were thinking about changing career. I wondered if you were serious or not.'

'I suppose that rather depends on what I'd be changing *to*,' said Kate. 'Did you have something in mind?'

'Housekeeper,' he said.

Kate laughed. 'You're not serious!'

'Why wouldn't I be?'

'You know how messy I am,' she said, still smiling. 'And you saw the state of our kitchen on Sunday. I'd have thought I'd be the last person you'd want as a housekeeper!'

'Tidiness isn't important. The fact that Alex likes you is.' Finn got up abruptly and began pacing around the office. 'She doesn't like many people. What I really need is someone who can meet her from school and keep an eye on her until I get home. You can cook, too, which is a bonus.'

Narrowly avoiding stepping on Derek who was stretched out in the middle of the floor, Finn muttered something under his breath and turned back to Kate. 'You could also look after that dog,' he pointed out crossly. 'I think we might as well forget the fiction that Alex is ever going to let you take him to your parents, so it looks as if I'm stuck with him, and I don't think Alison is going to be that keen on a dog in the office.'

'What about Rosa?' Kate asked. 'Isn't she coming back?'

'She rang last night. Her mother is going to need her full time for the foreseeable future. I told her I would make temporary arrangements, so that if she was in a position to come back in a couple of months, she could if she wanted to, but I don't think she will.'

'So you're not thinking about a permanent post?'

Finn shook his head. 'No. Alex isn't keen on anyone else living with us, so I might see if we can manage without a housekeeper—although it's going to be a lot more difficult now there's a dog to consider,' he added.

'Then why are you asking me?' Kate asked, ignoring that little sideswipe.

He stopped pacing and shoved his hands in his pockets. 'Because my sister's coming in a couple of weeks.'

Ah, yes, the scary Stella, Kate remembered.

'She'll just make a fuss if we haven't got anyone to help,' Finn went on, unaware of her mental interruption. 'It would just be for while she's here, so we're not talking about you staying for ever. That's why I thought if you didn't have anything else organised you might consider it. I'd pay you, of course,' he added. 'It would be more than you would make temping like this.'

Kate scribbled mindlessly on her notebook as she thought about Finn's offer. She had never been a big career girl, and had fallen into secretarial work simply because she couldn't think of anything else to do.

Phoebe and Bella were much more serious about their work, but deep down Kate was still nursing the childhood fantasy of living in a cottage in the country with a kitchen where she could make jam and bottle things, roses round the door and a big garden with room for lots of animals and children. Being a housekeeper might not be quite what she'd had in mind, but she was sure she'd be happy pottering around a house all day.

The more she thought about it, the more appealing the idea became. The money would be useful for a start, and a guaranteed job was better than hanging around waiting for the agency to get back to her.

Besides, she liked Alex and she liked Derek. The fact that she would be spending more time with Finn himself was just incidental, and had absolutely nothing to do with the flutter of anticipation that was stirring deep inside her.

She moistened her lips, striving to sound businesslike. 'Would it be a live-in post?'

'Preferably,' said Finn.

'I'd have to check with Bella,' said Kate, looking doubtful. 'It would mean she would be the only one in the house.'

'I'd cover the cost of your rent if you wanted to be sure of keeping your room,' he said unexpectedly, and she glanced at him in surprise.

'The rent's not such a problem since Phoebe married Gib,' she said frankly. 'There's nothing like a lovely, rich husband to stop you worrying about mortgages! Bella and I just pay a token rent now and look after the house for her. No, I was thinking about the cat.'

'The cat?' repeated Finn as if he didn't want to believe what he was hearing.

'I'd have to ask Bella to look after him, and he's bitten her ankles so many times she might not be that keen! Unless I could bring him with me?' Kate looked at Finn hopefully but he wasn't having any of it.

'No,' he said firmly. 'The dog is enough trouble. I'm sure Bella would feed the cat for you. It's not as if it would be for ever. Stella usually spends a couple of weeks with us, then travels around the country visiting her old friends for ten days or so, before coming back for the last few days before she flies back to Canada, so I don't anticipate needing you for longer than a month or so.'

Well, that told her. Lucky she hadn't done anything silly like falling in love with him, wasn't it?

Kate chewed the end of her pen. There was no point in feeling hurt that Finn wanted a definite time limit to the time she would be spending with him. He was just being practical, and she should be the same.

Did she really want to be a housekeeper?

If nothing else, it would be a change, she told herself. It might be fun. It would be money. It wasn't for ever, as Finn had been so keen to point out.

It would mean that she didn't have to say goodbye to him at the end of today.

'All right,' she said, suddenly making up her mind.

'You'll do it?' Finn sounded almost as surprised as she felt.

'Yes.' She would have to clear the cat feeding with Bella, who would grumble like mad, but she would agree in the end. In the meantime, it was up to Kate to make it very clear that she was going to be as businesslike as Finn.

'When do you want me?' she asked briskly, only to hear the double meaning in her words too late. 'To start,' she added, colour creeping into her cheeks.

So much for sounding businesslike.

Fortunately, Finn didn't appear to have noticed. 'Perhaps we can discuss the details over dinner?' he said stiltedly. 'Are you free tonight?'

'Yes,' said Kate, ruthlessly sacrificing the opportunity to meet lots of Will's single friends at a party. She would ring Bella and explain that she couldn't make it. Making chit-chat with a lot of corporate types at a noisy party couldn't compare to dinner with Finn, even if it was only to talk about her duties as housekeeper.

'Good.' Finn seemed rather at a loss. 'Could you book a restaurant?'

'Did you have somewhere in mind?' she asked, trying not to sound put out. It wasn't exactly a romantic date if you had to book your own restaurant, was it? Perhaps she should just order a pizza to be delivered and be done with it.

'You choose,' said Finn indifferently, turning away to the window.

Serve him right if she booked a table at the Dorchester, thought Kate, getting to her feet once more. Finn was still staring abstractedly at the rain, so it looked as if her interview was over.

'Book somewhere nice,' he said as she reached the door. 'There's something I want to ask you.'

'Something he wants to ask you?' Bella repeated when Kate recounted the conversation that evening. 'He didn't say what?'

'It'll be something to do with being house-keeper, I suppose.'

'Come on, Kate!' Bella rolled her eyes dismissively. 'You don't invite a girl like you out to dinner to talk about how many hours you're going to spend vacuuming!' She paused. 'Maybe he's going to make a pass?'

'I don't think that's very likely,' said Kate, unwilling to admit to Bella that she had already wondered about this possibility and been unable to imagine Finn doing anything of the kind. 'He's had plenty of opportunity to do that without wasting money on a meal.'

'Ah, but you've been working for him up to now,' Bella pointed out. 'He sounds the sort of strait-laced type who doesn't approve of office affairs, but he might have been nurturing a secret passion for you for weeks, and now that he's got a window of opportunity this weekend when you're technically unemployed he's decided to go for it!'

Kate pooh-poohed the idea, of course, but it didn't stop her stomach churning with nerves as she got ready that evening. She had booked the Italian restaurant round the corner, not that she thought that she would be able to eat anything. Bella told her she should have gone for somewhere more expensive, but Kate didn't want Finn to think that she was expecting anything special. Best just to treat it as a business meeting, she had decided.

Which made it difficult to decide what to wear. He had seen all her work clothes and, even though it clearly wasn't a proper date, Kate couldn't help wanting him to see that she could look nice when she tried. At length she settled on a short, flirty little dress with a beaded cardigan and her favourite shoes. They weren't very suitable for walking through a dank March night, but she didn't have anything else that would go.

'You look great,' said Bella when Kate went downstairs. 'Not at all like a housekeeper.'

Kate immediately lost her nerve. Perhaps it *was* a bit inappropriate. 'Do you think I should change?'

'Into what?' Bella was appalled at the very idea. 'A demure grey dress with a white collar and a load of keys hanging from your waist? Of course don't change! You look fabulous as you are. Finn won't be able to keep his hands off you!'

For once Bella was quite wrong. Finn didn't seem to be having any trouble at all keeping his hands to himself, Kate reflected dismally as they struggled to make stilted conversation on the way to the restaurant. He had certainly noted her change of image, and he had looked a bit taken aback, but all he had said was that she looked 'different'. As compliments went, it was hardly overwhelming.

Finn obviously wasn't over-impressed by the restaurant either. Tough, thought Kate. He should have organised somewhere himself. He ought to count himself lucky that she hadn't taken up Bella's suggestion of booking a table at Claridge's.

'Is this it?' he said, looking around him at the red and white checked tablecloths, the faded posters on the wall and the candles stuck into Chianti bottles. The last word in style in the Sixties.

'I'm a cheap date,' said Kate defiantly, and then, when he lifted an eyebrow, lost her nerve. 'Not that this is a date, of course,' she added hastily.

Unfortunately the waiters hadn't got that particular message and kept fussing around them, promising them a secluded table and showering Kate with embarrassing compliments while a muscle in Finn's gritted jaw began to twitch. She wished they would all shut up. Any minute now a posse of violinists would pop up to serenade them, and there would be some pseudo-gipsy insisting that Finn bought her a rose at an exorbitant price.

'She is very beautiful, no?' The head waiter demanded, determined to foster what he thought was a budding romance.

Finn looked across at Kate, who was cringing, sinking further and further down into her seat. She looked so uncomfortable that his own rigid expression relaxed into something that was almost, but not quite, a smile.

'Yes,' he said. 'Very. Now, could we have a menu, please?'

Kate's cheeks burned. 'I'm sorry,' she said when the waiter had departed, still wreathed in smiles. 'They're not usually like this here.'

'Perhaps you don't usually look as beautiful as you do tonight,' said Finn, picking up the wine list.

Kate opened her mouth and closed it again, but before she could think of anything to say two waiters descended on them again and they were caught up in the kerfuffle of being offered menus and bread and having water poured, while her pulse boomed in her ears and her heart lurched around her chest.

Finn had said she was beautiful.

She risked a glance across at him. His head was bent over the wine list, and his expression was hard to read. From where she sat, he looked as if he was absorbed in the relative merits of Valpolicella and Lambrusco. The fierce, dark brows were drawn slightly together, and his eyes were shielded, so that all Kate could see was the strong nose and the line of his mouth.

Her entrails twisted at the sight, and she looked quickly away. She must have misheard. Nobody, not even Finn, could say something like that and then calmly turn his attention to what they were going to drink. He couldn't tell her that she was beautiful and then carry on as if nothing had happened, could he?

Could he?

Maybe he hadn't meant it. Maybe he had just said it to shut the waiter up. Kate's hands shook as she pretended to study her own menu, but the words danced in front of her eyes and she couldn't concentrate. *Did* he think that she was beautiful? Was Bella right after all?

At last they had ordered, the wine had been tasted and poured, and the last hovering waiter had backed off to leave them alone. Having longed for them to go away, Kate now wished they would come back. They might be annoying but at least they would break the uncomfortable silence that had fallen.

She fiddled with her fork. Finn seemed to have forgotten that he wanted to say something to her. Why had he bothered to ask her out if he didn't want to talk to her? 'When would you like me to start as housekeeper?' she asked eventually, unable to bear it any longer.

Finn had been tearing a piece of bread apart, but he looked up at that, as if relieved that she had started the conversational ball rolling. 'Whenever you can manage it,' he said. 'As soon as possible as far as Alex and I are concerned. It would give you a chance to get settled in before Stella arrives.'

'I could move this weekend if you wanted,' Kate offered.

'Good. In that case, we'll come and pick you up on Sunday,' said Finn, but he seemed abstracted, as if there was something else on his mind.

'When is your sister arriving?'

'Two weeks on Tuesday. We'll need to make a bit of a fuss of her when she arrives,' he added.

'That's all right, I'm good at fuss,' said Kate, feeling a bit more cheerful. 'I'll make everything special for her. Flowers in her room, fresh towels, luxury soap, a nice welcoming meal…we'll lay on the works for her!'

Finn raised his brows slightly. 'You sound like you've done this kind of thing before?'

'We always had lots of guests at home when I was growing up,' she told him. 'I love having people to stay too.'

'I'm afraid I'm a bit out of the way of it,' said Finn, turning his fork absently between his fingers. 'I haven't done any proper entertaining since Isabel died. Stella's the only person we've had to stay for any length of time.'

Their starters arrived just then. Kate waited until the plates had been deposited with a flourish in front of them.

'Is that what you wanted to talk to me about?'

Finn had picked up his knife and fork, but at that he laid them down again. 'Partly,' he said. 'At least...well, no, not really,' he finished abruptly.

'What is it?' asked Kate, puzzled.

'I don't quite know how you're going to take this...' Finn trailed off and she looked at him curiously. She had never seen him this nervous before.

'I won't know until you tell me,' she pointed out.

'No.' Finn drank some wine and set his glass down carefully. 'It's just that Stella rang the other day. You remember I told you that she was very keen to introduce me to women she thinks would make suitable stepmothers for Alex?'

'Yes,' Kate encouraged him when he seemed likely to stop again.

'Alex spoke to her first. Stella was telling her all about some friend of a friend of hers who she thought it would be nice for me to meet and why didn't she invite her to dinner one night, and I gather Alex didn't like the sound of her at all. So she told Stella that she didn't need to bother finding a stepmother for her any more because I'd met someone and was going to get married.'

'Oh, dear…'

'Exactly.' A mirthless smile twisted Finn's mouth. 'Of course, Stella then insisted on talking to me. I could have told her that Alex was joking, but they have quite an uneasy relationship as it is, and I didn't want Stella coming over and going on about how spoilt and difficult she was, which would just make Alex defensive. It was bad enough last time.'

Finn sighed. 'Anyway, the upshot was that I played along. I remembered what Alex had suggested that day we all went to Richmond Park, and I suppose I thought—well, why not? It would shut Stella up at least, although not initially. She demanded details of course, wanted to know the name of my fiancée, how we had met and so on.

There was an odd feeling in the pit of Kate's stomach. 'What did you tell her?'

Finn looked her straight in the eye. 'I told her it was you,' he said.

CHAPTER SEVEN

SHE should have been expecting it, but somehow she wasn't. Kate wrenched her eyes away from Finn's and looked down at her plate, appalled at the sudden realisation of how much she wished that he had meant what he said to his sister, that he loved her and wanted to marry her.

She felt very strange. It was as if all the oxygen had been sucked out of the air, leaving her light-headed and faintly dizzy, so that it took her a little while to realise what Finn was saying.

'I wanted to ask you if you would pretend that it was true.'

Pretend. Kate made herself focus on the one word that made all the difference. This wasn't her wishes coming miraculously true at all, it was Finn making it clear that he wasn't talking about anything real.

'I know it's not fair on you, and that it's a lot to ask, but it would mean a lot to Alex. And to me,' he added after a moment. 'Of course, it would just be a pretence,' he hastened to explain when Kate said nothing but just sat staring dumbly at him. 'I wouldn't expect you to...to think of it as anything other than a job.'

'A job?' Kate latched onto the word as if it was the only one she had understood. Her heart was thudding so loudly that it was hard to hear, and she was afraid she might miss something important.

'I wouldn't ask you to do something like that for free,' said Finn. 'I'd make it worth your while financially. We could agree your salary as housekeeper with a bonus on top of that at the end for...everything else.'

He spoke very formally, making it clear that as far as he was concerned it would be a purely business transaction, and somehow Kate managed to pull herself together.

'What exactly would you want me to do?' she asked, amazed at the calmness of her voice.

'To be around when Stella is with us. To make her believe that you and I...'

'Are in love?' Kate finished for him bravely when he hesitated.

Finn let out a breath. 'Yes.'

'I used to be good at drama,' she said after a moment. 'I always wanted a starring role but only ever got bit parts, so perhaps I could look on this as my chance to get back into acting.'

'You mean you will consider it?' he said as if he could hardly believe that she was serious.

'Why not?' Kate had herself under control now.

The one thing she mustn't do was let Finn guess that she had fallen in love with him. He would be appalled if he knew, and he certainly wouldn't ask her to pretend to be his fiancée. Convincing him that she was treating the whole thing lightly would at least let her be near him, Kate told herself. It might not be for long, but it could be her only chance.

'It will be much more fun than temping, anyway,' she told him brightly. 'It sounds like easy money to me!'

'You might not think so when you meet my sister,' said Finn with a wry look. 'She has very sharp eyes and she isn't a fool. She'll be watching us very carefully.' He paused delicately. 'If we're going to convince her that we really are engaged, we might have to give the impression that we're more intimate than we really are.'

Treat it lightly, Kate reminded herself. 'You mean we might have to kiss occasionally?'

'That kind of thing, yes.' Finn seemed a little nonplussed by her casual attitude. 'How would you feel about that?'

How would she feel? Kate let herself imagine being able to reach across the table and take his hand. She imagined putting her arms around him and leaning into his solidity, daring to touch her lips to his throat. She thought about being held by him and how that stern mouth would feel against hers, and desire knotted sharply inside her, driving the breath from her lungs.

'I think I could manage.' She meant to say it casually, but her voice came out treacherously husky and she had to clear her throat and start again. 'It would just be part of the job. It wouldn't mean anything.'

'Right,' said Finn, sounding oddly wary, and Kate was suddenly terrified in case he had glimpsed how badly she wanted him.

'I'll close my eyes and think of the bonus,' she tried to joke.

'Yes, I think I've got the point that you won't be taking it seriously.' There was a distinct edge to Finn's voice now, and Kate eyed him uncertainly.

What had she said? She'd have thought he would have been glad that she wasn't going to go all soppy on him! Kate sighed inwardly, torn between exasperation at the withdrawn look on his face and the longing to reach for him and tell him that all she wanted was to hold him and kiss him and be with him for ever, and you couldn't get more serious than that.

'How does Alex feel about all of this?' she asked instead.

Finn's rigid expression relaxed slightly. 'She's very pleased with herself, taking credit for the whole idea. I told her I was going to ask you if you'd play along tonight, so she'll be cock-a-hoop when she hears that you've agreed.' He glanced across the table at Kate. 'Alex doesn't take to many people, but she likes you.'

'I like her too.'

There was a pause while the obvious question—And what about you? Do *you* like me?—seemed to shimmer in the air between them.

Kate swallowed the words. She wasn't going to ask Finn that. Her eyes fell on her starter, forgotten and growing cold in front of her. She wasn't hungry—love seemed to have destroyed her appetite—but she picked up her fork and began to eat while the silence stretched uncomfortably.

'What have you told Stella about me?' she asked with a kind of desperation at last.

'Just your name and that we met when you came to work with me.' Finn didn't seem to be enjoying his meal any more than she was. 'I thought it would be easiest if I stuck to the truth as far as possible.'

'I bet she wanted to know more than that,' said Kate. 'If my brother told me that he was getting married, I would demand to know every last detail!'

A faint smile of acknowledgment lifted the corners of his mouth. 'She did ask what you were like,' he admitted.

'What did you tell her?'

Finn looked at Kate with an unreadable expression. 'That you were warm and funny and kind, and that Alex liked you. Which is true.'

What was true? That Alex liked her, or that he thought that she was warm and funny?

Kind. Warm. There was nothing wrong with being either, but it was hardly sweep-you-off-your-feet stuff, was it? Kate pushed her mushrooms glumly around her plate. She wanted him to have described her to Stella in rather more lover-like terms. Beautiful. Desirable.

Irresistible. How come none of those words had popped into his head when he thought about her?

She knew why.

Because Finn didn't think she was beautiful or desirable, and he could resist her quite easily.

Because he didn't love her.

She was just going to have to live with that.

Kate laid down her fork, unable to face any more. 'Didn't Stella want to know what had made you change your mind about getting married?'

'I said that she would understand when she met you,' said Finn.

Their eyes met across the candle in the middle of the table, and something leapt in the air between them, something that jarred Kate's heart and was gone before she could tell what it was.

She moistened her lips. 'What would you have done if I'd said no?'

'I'm not sure,' he admitted. 'I was relying on your kindness. I suppose I could always have pretended that you'd left me for someone else just before she arrived.'

'I wouldn't do anything like that!' Kate protested involuntarily, and that keen grey glance flickered to her face and then away before she could read his expression again.

'No, maybe you wouldn't,' he agreed.

'You could always have invented some family crisis,' she offered helpfully.

'It would take more than a family crisis to stop Stella,' said Finn. 'She'd track you down somehow!'

'Anyway, I didn't say no,' Kate pointed out.

'No.' Finn abandoned his own plate. 'We'll have to think of some reason to end our supposed engagement after Stella leaves though, or she'll be booking her ticket back to the wedding. As it is, we'll be lucky if we get away with not getting married while she's here! Oh, don't worry,' he added, misinterpreting Kate's flinch. 'It won't go that far!'

'Good.' Kate managed a weak smile. 'We don't want that, do we?'

'No,' Finn agreed, his voice empty of expression. 'We don't want that.'

'Are you sure this is a good idea, Kate?' Bella and Phoebe, sitting across the table from her like an interviewing panel, looked at her in concern.

'Earning money is always a good idea, isn't it?' said Kate defiantly.

'There are easier ways to earn it than pretending to be in love with your boss!'

'Oh, I don't know...'

Kate didn't want to tell them that the problem was going to be a whole lot more complicated than that. She was going to have to pretend to be in love with Finn while pretending not to be. No point in explaining that to them, though. Bella would only say 'I told you so.'

'It'll be better than temping in some dreary office,' she told them instead, 'and Finn's going to give me a huge bonus for the engagement thing which will mean I can clear my credit card bill. I might even have some left to save up for a holiday. Besides, I like Alex and it solves the problem of what to do about Derek during the day.'

'Oh, well, that's all right then!' said Bella sarcastically. 'As long as the *dog* is sorted out...!'

'Look, it will be fine! I don't know why you're both making such a fuss. It's just a job.'

'Just a job where you have to sleep with your boss!'

'I'll have my own room.'

Phoebe looked dubious. 'His sister's not going to believe you're going to get married if you're not even sleeping together.'

'Well...we can say it doesn't seem appropriate with Alex in the house,' said Kate a little defensively.

Bella pretended to shake her head and look disorientated. 'Sorry, I seem to have stepped into a time warp! What year are we living in?'

Kate ignored her. 'OK, so we'll share a room when his sister is there. It's not a big deal.'

'We just don't want you to get hurt,' Phoebe tried to placate her, hearing the edge in Kate's voice.

'I'm not going to do anything silly,' said Kate grittily. It was too late now, anyway, although she had no intention of confessing *that*!

'Finn's still in love with Isabel, I know that. Even if he wasn't still obsessed by her, he's completely different from me. He's much older, his experience is different, his life is different.'

All true, and it didn't make the slightest difference to loving him.

Kate faced her friends squarely, marvelling that they couldn't see how different *she* felt now. Couldn't they tell that falling in love with

Finn had turned her life upside down, consuming her to the point where she was prepared to risk the certainty of being hurt just to be with him?

'There's no point in me getting involved with him or his daughter or his dog,' she told them, knowing that was true too but unable to do anything about it. 'But it's not like I've got anything else lined up that I can do instead,' she pointed out. 'It's that or hang around waiting for the agency to get in touch. Frankly, I'd rather be paid generously for living in a comfortable house for a few weeks!'

Phoebe was unconvinced. 'It's very easy to get carried away in situations like that,' she said. 'And I should know!'

'Yes, you're the last person who should be advising Kate against a mock engagement,' said Bella with a grin. 'Look where it got you and Gib!'

Phoebe smiled, but her eyes were serious as she glanced across at Kate. 'Finn's not like Gib,' she said. 'I just think you should be careful, that's all.'

Too late, thought Kate. All she could do now was make the best of the time she had.

*　　*　　*

'This is your room.' Alex opened the door and showed Kate inside proudly. 'I made it look nice for you.'

Kate looked around her, touched. 'It all looks lovely,' she said. There was even a little vase of flowers on the chest of drawers. 'Did you do it all yourself?'

'Dad made your bed,' Alex admitted, 'but I did everything else.'

Kate looked at the bed and imagined Finn making it, smoothing his hand over the sheet where she would lie. Shaken by a gust of longing, she cleared her throat. 'That was nice of him, but I could have made it myself.'

'I don't think he minded,' said Alex casually. 'Do you want to see my room?'

Maybe that would be safer.

Kate admired Alex's room and was suitably appreciative of the fact that it had been specially tidied for the occasion. A pinboard by her bed was covered in photographs, of Alex and her mother and of Finn. Most of them showed him with Isabel, smiling and relaxed with the sun in his eyes, and Kate felt hollow inside to realise that she had never seen him look happy like that.

Might never see him looking happy.

'That's my mum,' said Alex, following Kate's gaze. 'She was beautiful, wasn't she?'

'Yes,' said Kate. 'She was. Do you remember her at all?'

'Not really, but Dad tells me about her and he kept some of her things for me. Look.' Alex dived under her bed for a box which she pulled out and opened reverently.

Kate sat on the bed and took the things Alex handed her. A lipstick, used. A bottle of perfume, half full. A soft silk scarf. A book of medieval poetry. A diary full of scribbled notes. A pair of earrings. A baby's footprint.

'That was mine,' said Alex.

There was a hard lump in Kate's throat as she thought about Finn carefully choosing the things that would give her the sense of what her mother had been like long after she had gone. It must have broken his heart all over again.

'This was her engagement ring,' Alex said, opening a little jewellery box and pointing at one of the rings. 'Dad says she left it to me, so I can wear it later if I want to. Those blue stones are called sapphires. Dad bought that ring because they reminded him of Mum's eyes.'

'It's a lovely ring,' said Kate, perilously close to tears. Her heart ached for Finn, but she didn't want to break down and weep in front of Alex.

She looked up from the box instead only to find Finn watching her gravely from the doorway. For a long, long moment, they looked at each other, Kate's brown eyes, shimmering with tears, before Alex noticed her father and jumped up.

'I'm showing Kate Mum's box,' she said.

'So I see.' Finn's smile looked strained, but all he said was that he had made some tea if they wanted to come downstairs.

Kate felt awful, as if she had been caught nosing around in his private memories but when she tried to apologise while Alex was carefully putting the box back under her bed, he brushed it aside.

'I'm glad she wanted to talk about Isabel,' he said, handing Kate a mug of tea. 'I don't think she's ever shown anyone that box before. She's always kept her feelings to herself, and it's difficult to get her to talk about what's worrying her sometimes. If you can get her to talk to you, I'd be very grateful. She's already much chattier than she used to be.'

As if to prove his point, Alex came clattering down the stairs with Derek and burst into the kitchen. 'Dad, I've just thought of something when I was putting Mum's ring away. Kate should have a ring too if she's going to be your fiancée, shouldn't she?'

'Oh, no…no, there's no need for that,' said Kate hastily. She held up her hand to show the rings she was wearing. 'I could use one of these.'

Finn took her hand as if it were a parcel, and he and Alex inspected her meagre display of rings. Neither of them was impressed.

'I don't think any of them are likely to convince Stella,' said Finn, looking down his nose. 'Let me have that one,' he said, pointing to the one on her third finger.

Kate's hand was burning where he had touched her as she tugged off the ring. 'What for?' she asked.

'It'll give me your size. I'll get you a proper ring.'

'Really, I don't think it's necessary—' she began, but he interrupted her.

'You don't know my sister. She'd smell a rat if you were wearing a cheap little ring like that. Why are you looking like that?' he demanded, his voice sharpening at the involuntary change in Kate's expression.

'Seb gave me that ring.' The fact that Finn had instantly recognised it as cheap made Kate realise at last just how little Seb had valued her. She had treasured the ring, so certain that the fact that he had given her one at all meant that he cared, but all along it had been worthless, just like Seb.

Finn frowned. 'I won't lose it.'

'It doesn't matter. I don't think I want to wear it again.' Kate summoned a bright smile and got to her feet. 'I'd better start thinking about supper.'

Finn was all for getting a take-away, but Kate was determined to show him that she hadn't forgotten why she was there. 'I may as well start earning my salary,' she said.

There wasn't a lot in the fridge, but she found enough to make a sauce for some pasta. It seemed very ordinary fare to her but Finn and Alex carried on as if she had produced something worthy of a Michelin star.

'I think you've been having too many take-aways,' said Kate. 'That's all going to change!'

By half past eight, Alex was wilting. 'Time for bed, young lady,' said Finn. 'You've got school tomorrow.'

Ensuring that she had cleaned her teeth, kissing her goodnight and dealing firmly with her last-ditch attempts to delay the moment of lights out took some time, and then there was the washing up and tidying to do, but after that Finn and Kate had no excuse not to realise that they were alone with the dog.

By tacit agreement, they stayed in the bright, safe light of the kitchen rather than retreat to the comfort and intimate shadows of the sitting room. Kate sat on the other side of the kitchen table from Finn, where there was no danger of brushing against him by mistake.

Now all she had to do was chat brightly to break the yawning silence, but she couldn't think of a single thing to say. All she could think about was Finn sitting on the other side of the table, about his mouth and his hands and how nice it would be to be able to get up and go round to sit on his lap, to put her arms around his neck and kiss the tiredness from his face.

In the end it was Finn who spoke first. 'I hope you're all right with this,' he said, lifting his eyes to fix Kate with that disturbingly acute grey gaze. 'I mean...with the situation.'

'Of course,' said Kate brightly, as if she hadn't given the fact that they were alone together with only the dog as chaperon a moment's thought.

Finn looked around the kitchen as if trying to see it through her eyes. 'A job like this isn't much fun for a girl like you.'

'That rather depends on what kind of girl you think I am,' she said.

He considered the matter seriously. 'I suppose I think of you as someone who likes to have a good time,' he said eventually. 'You seem to have lots of friends, and you're always out. I can't help feeling that you might find it a bit dull stuck in the house all day.'

'It'll be a lot more fun that being stuck in an office,' said Kate. 'I've always liked pottering around the house. I'm not the tidiest person in the world—as you know!' she added seeing the sardonic lift of Finn's brows. 'But I love cooking and sewing and gardening and if I've got a dog to walk and Alex to chat to when she gets home from school...well, I think I'm going to have a lovely time. In fact, I don't know why I didn't think about being a housekeeper before,' she finished.

'You know, you're not a bad PA when you concentrate,' said Finn carefully. 'I'm sure you could have a more interesting career than housekeeping if you applied yourself.'

Kate turned her glass between her fingers on the table. 'I don't really want to,' she said frankly. 'The trouble is that I haven't got any ambition.'

'What, none?'

'Only for very ordinary things,' she said. 'It seems a bit shameful to admit it, but all I've ever really wanted was to find someone special. To have children and a house I could make a home. That's not asking too much, is it?'

Finn's expression was unreadable. 'No.'

'Phoebe and Bella think it would be boring, but I'd be so happy keeping chickens and making jam and helping out at the school fête.' Kate sighed a little. 'That's partly why I was so broken up about Seb. I'd made myself believe that he was the one, and that I could have that dream with him.

'I was stupid, of course,' she went on, keeping her eyes on her glass, not looking at Finn. 'Seb wouldn't be seen dead at a school fête and he doesn't care where his eggs come from. It made it worse when I had to accept that. It's like giving up on a dream of what my life might be like as well as giving up on him.'

'Dreams are hard things to let go of,' said Finn quietly.

Kate knew he was thinking of his dead wife, and her throat tightened. 'Is that what you had with Isabel? The dream?'

He lifted his shoulders slightly. 'It feels like a dream now,' he told her. 'I'm sure it can't have been that perfect and that we must have argued sometimes, but I don't remember that. I just remember how special it was to be with her.'

'You're lucky to have had that.' Kate stopped, hearing her words too late. 'I'm sorry,' she said. 'That was tactless of me. You probably don't feel very lucky.'

'I know what you mean,' said Finn with a faint smile. 'And in a lot of ways I was lucky. A lot of people never find what Isabel and I had. Sometimes I can't believe I found love like that once, and the statistics are against me finding it a second time. It's just not going to happen.'

His mouth twisted. 'That's when I miss Isabel most,' he told Kate. 'When I remember how completely happy I was with her and know that I'm never going to have that again.'

That night Kate lay in bed and stared up at the dark ceiling, thinking about the expression in Finn's eyes. It was terrible to feel envious of someone who was dead, but she couldn't stop thinking about Isabel and how much Finn had loved her.

'It's not going to happen a second time,' he had said, and she would have to accept that, too. It was no use dreaming that she might become his second chance at happiness. The statistics were against it, weren't they?

Kate's heart cracked and she squeezed her eyes shut. What was wrong with her? Why did she keep falling in love with men who couldn't, or wouldn't, ever love her back?

This job had offered her the chance to be with him and she had jumped at it, but now Kate wondered if it had been such a good idea. It wasn't as if she hadn't always known that falling in love with Finn was hopeless. It might have been better to have said goodbye and walked away while she still could.

But it was too late for that now. She was just going to have to get on with it, Kate told herself. If she couldn't make Finn happy, she could at least try to make him comfortable for a while, and if pretending to be his fiancée would make his life easier during his sister's visit, then she would do that too.

It felt odd not to be going into the office to be with Finn the next day, but having made her decision, Kate was quite as happy as she had said she would be pottering around the house. She took Alex to school and, by the time she had walked the dog, cleaned the house, inspected the cupboards and done the shopping, and walked the dog again, it was time to pick Alex up.

When Finn came home that evening, the two of them were in the kitchen. Kate was in the middle of making supper and Alex was sitting at the kitchen table doing her homework.

Finn bent to kiss his daughter, and then looked at Kate, who had the dizzy feeling that the obvious thing for him to do next was to walk across and kiss her too. She turned firmly back to her sauce.

'How was your day?' she asked, grimacing at the corniness of it. Any minute now she would be offering to bring him his pipe and slippers!

'Fine.' There was a faint frown between Finn's brows as if he was remembering something that hadn't been fine at all. 'Busy.'

'How was Alison?' Kate made herself ask.

'She was…fine.'

Fine was obviously the key word for the day. Finn wrenched at his tie to loosen it.

'You didn't miss me then?' she said, making a joke out of it.

'Funnily enough, I did.'

Kate's heart stumbled, and without thinking she turned to face him. 'Really?' she said, still clutching her wooden spoon.

'Really,' said Finn.

His eyes seemed to reach right inside her and squeeze her heart until Kate's breathing got into a muddle and she forgot whether she was supposed to be breathing in or breathing out.

He had missed her. He wasn't just saying it, he had really missed her! OK, it wasn't a fraction of what he still felt for Isabel but, as Kate stared back at him, unable to tear her eyes away from that piercing grey gaze, she told herself that it was enough.

There was a long, long pause. Kate could feel the air shortening even as silence lengthened, and when the phone rang jarringly she actually jumped and dropped the wooden spoon.

Her hands were unsteady as she washed it under the tap.

Alex had pounced on phone. 'Oh, hello, Aunt Stella,' she said, and for the next few minutes dutifully answered questions about school. 'Yes, he's here,' she said after a while, and then, ultra-casual, 'He's just talking to Kate.'

She beamed at Finn as she held the phone out to him. He took it, visibly bracing himself. Stirring her sauce intently, Kate could hear only one side of the conversation, which seemed to consist of a lot of talking on Stella's part and brief replies on his.

'No, you can't talk to her,' she heard him say eventually. 'I don't want you interrogating her over the phone... You can meet her when you come... No, we're not planning on getting married while you're here. There's no rush. Kate's living here now and we're all perfectly happy as we are.'

Shaking his head, Finn put down the phone. 'My sister...!' He turned to Kate who was still concentrating fiercely on her sauce. 'Well, it looks as if we're committed now,' he said. 'I hope you don't want to change your mind?'

'No.' Kate took the saucepan off the heat and turned off the element. 'I won't change my mind.'

'Good.' Finn walked over to where she was standing by the cooker. 'Give me your hand. No, not that one,' he said as he pulled a box out of his jacket pocket. 'The other one.'

Kate had to steel herself against the shiver of response that shuddered through her as he took her left hand and turned it over, spreading it so that he could slide a ring onto her third finger.

'What do you think?'

If she hadn't known better, Kate could have sworn that he was nervous about her answer. She looked down at her hand. He seemed to have forgotten that he was still holding it and she was excruciatingly conscious of the warmth of his fingers.

She made herself focus on the ring. It was an antique, a cluster of pearls around a topaz on warm old gold. 'It's beautiful,' she said with difficulty.

Alex was less impressed. She peered round her father, studying the ring critically. 'It ought to be diamonds, Dad,' she said severely.

'Diamonds wouldn't be right for Kate.' Finn seemed to remember that he was still holding Kate's hand and let it go abruptly. 'They're too cold.'

Kate bit her lip as she twisted the ring on her finger. 'It must have been terribly expensive,' she said worriedly.

'It will be worth it if it shuts Stella up,' said Finn, stepping back.

There was a pause. 'Do you really like it?' he asked as if the words had been forced out of him

'I love it,' she said honestly.

'I could get you a diamond ring if you'd rather.'

'I don't want diamonds,' said Kate. She risked a glance at him, and the light in her eyes turned them almost exactly the colour of the topaz. 'This is perfect.'

CHAPTER EIGHT

ALEX refused to be convinced. 'I still think it should be a diamond ring,' she said stubbornly. 'If Aunt Stella sees that old thing she might think you don't love Kate.'

Kate looked down at her beautiful ring. *That old thing?*

Finn was regarding his daughter with some exasperation. 'We'll just have to make her believe that I do anyway.'

'How?'

'Well...I'll tell her that I do.'

'I don't think that will be enough for Aunt Stella,' said Alex, making a face. 'You know what she's like.'

'I'm sure we'll think of something to convince her,' said Finn, and tried to change the subject by suggesting that she laid the table for supper.

Alex was not to be so easily diverted. 'I think you might have to kiss Kate,' she said as she set out the knives and forks.

'Possibly,' he said repressively.

Kate busied herself draining potatoes and avoided looking at either of them.

'Have you ever kissed her?' Alex asked her father with interest.

There was a frozen pause. 'I don't think that's any of your business, Alex,' he said in a curt voice.

It didn't seem to have much effect on Alex. 'I only thought you might need to practise if you haven't,' she said, all injured innocence.

'Well, we're not going to practise now,' Finn said with a something of a snap. 'We're going to have supper instead, and then *you* are going to bed!'

Only Alex seemed unaware of the air of constraint in the kitchen. She chattered on and Kate smiled mechanically and thought about kissing Finn. She wouldn't mind if it was just a practice. It would still be a kiss.

Please, please let him kiss me, she prayed.

She cleared up in the kitchen automatically while Finn was saying goodnight to Alex. She mustn't seem too keen. If he suggested taking Alex up on her idea, she would pretend to think about it and then agree casually.

Only Finn didn't suggest it. He made no reference to Stella's visit or Alex's conversation or anything at all that might give Kate an opening. He just helped her tidy up, moving efficiently and expressionlessly around the kitchen without once coming anywhere near her.

Frustrated, Kate wondered if she dared raise the subject herself. She didn't think she would have the nerve at first but, as the silence lengthened uncomfortably, she changed her mind. Dammit, they were both supposed to be grown-ups here! Why *shouldn't* she say something? It was exactly the kind of thing she ought to be able to discuss if she was treating this purely as a job.

Folding a tea towel and picking up some plates, Kate took the plunge. 'I've been thinking about what Alex said.'

'Which particular thing?' Finn asked. He was putting glasses back in the cupboard and sounding abstracted, as if he was thinking about something else entirely. 'I can't believe I used to worry that she was too quiet,' he added. 'She never shuts up now.'

Kate eyed his back with some resentment. He obviously wasn't going to make it easy for her!

'We were talking about your sister's visit,' she prompted him, and Finn turned, grey eyes suddenly alert.

'Ah.'

'Alex suggested that it might be an idea to practise a kiss before Stella arrives,' said Kate, amazed at how calm she sounded.

'And what do you think?' asked Finn.

To her outrage, there was an undercurrent of something that might have been amusement, or possibly surprise. Whatever it was, it was enough to make Kate put up her chin and clutch the plates she was carrying defensively to her chest.

'I think we should,' she said coldly. 'There's no point in this elaborate charade if we're going to look as if we've never touched each other before. If your sister is as shrewd as you say she is, she'll see that we're uncomfortable together and it won't take her long to guess that we're not really engaged at all.'

'I suppose you're right,' Finn admitted grudgingly.

Kate's lips tightened. That's it, make it sound like kissing her would be a tiresome chore he'd really rather get out of!

'It's not going to be easy for either of us,' she said sharply, annoyed with him and even more annoyed with herself for wanting him even when he was making her cross. 'I just think it would be a lot less embarrassing if we don't have to kiss for the first time in front of an interested audience.'

Finn put the last glass away and closed the cupboard door. 'So you want me to kiss you?'

Yes.

'I don't *want* you to kiss me,' lied Kate with a frosty look. 'I'm merely suggesting that it might be sensible if we practised kissing each other in advance so it's not too awkward when we have to convince your sister.'

'OK,' said Finn. 'Shall we do it now?'

'Now?' faltered Kate. Having won her point, she was unprepared for him to follow it up quite so quickly.

'We might as well get it over with.'

Charming! But she was the one trying to convince him that it was just a job as far as she was concerned, Kate acknowledged reluctantly. She could hardly turn round now and demand a romantic setting or a more intimate moment.

She swallowed. 'All right.'

Finn came over and took the plates from her nerveless hands. He put them on the table and turned back to where Kate stood, her pulse booming thunderously in her ears and her knees treacherously weak.

'Shall we do it then?' he asked, unsmiling.

Her throat was so dry that Kate couldn't speak. She nodded dumbly instead, and Finn took her by the waist to draw her slightly closer. Trying to anticipate and make it easier for him, Kate tilted up her face as he bent his head, but they ended up bumping noses and he released her awkwardly.

'It's just as well we're practising,' she said huskily, trying to laugh but not really succeeding.

'Just as well,' Finn agreed. 'Shall we try again?'

'OK.'

This time, he put his hands on her arms and slid them slowly to her shoulders as he looked down into her eyes almost thoughtfully. Locked into that cool, grey gaze, Kate stood mouse-still while he cupped her face between his warm hands. She was quivering with anticipation, and there was a fluttery feeling of excitement beneath her skin that jolted as Finn bent his head towards hers once more.

It was a better kiss this time. Much better. So much better, in fact, that Kate felt the floor drop away beneath her feet as his mouth touched hers. She put her hands out to steady herself against him, and he kissed her again and then things got a bit confused.

Afterwards, Kate wasn't sure how it had happened, but one moment she was standing there being controlled—relatively, anyway— and the next her arms were sliding round his waist, and she was melting into him, holding him, kissing him back.

Finn's fingers had drifted from her cheeks and were tangled in her hair. Kate had always thought of his mouth as being cool and stern, even hard, but it didn't feel like that now. It was warm and persuasive against hers, and it felt so right that she stopped thinking at all and gave herself up to the heady pleasure of kissing and being kissed while the tiny tremor of excitement inside her grew stronger and stronger, feeding on the touch of his lips and the taste of his mouth and the feel of his hard, solid body against hers, until it overwhelmed that gentle, reassuring rightness and spun Kate out of control.

She clung to Finn, half thrilled, half terrified by the intensity of it, not knowing how to break the kiss, not wanting to, but afraid that unless she did there would be no way she could keep him from knowing how she really felt.

Perhaps Finn sensed her confusion, or perhaps he too was alarmed by how quickly the brief practise kiss had taken on a life of its own, swamping their sensible intentions and sweeping them into uncharted territory, for he hesitated and then, with difficulty, lifted his head.

There was a long, long moment when they just stared shakily at each other, and then he seemed to realise that his fingers were still entwined in her soft, brown curls, and he pulled his hands abruptly away.

Kate was left reeling. It was all she could do to stay upright. She was dizzy and disorientated, and her heart was pumping with something close to terror at how badly she wanted to throw herself back into Finn's arms and beg him to kiss her again.

Finn was looking aghast, and he stepped back as if afraid that she would do just that.

'Well...' he said, and then hesitated, evidently not knowing what else to say.

'That...that was better,' Kate managed unsteadily. The appalled expression on Finn's face was enough to bring her crashing back to earth. So much for dreams when all it took was a single kiss to make the scales fall from his eyes and persuade him that he might be able to love her after all.

All she could do now, Kate decided, was try and treat it lightly and whatever she did, not let him guess how much kissing him had meant to her. She wasn't sure she could pretend to have hated it as much as he obviously had, but she could at least reassure him that she wasn't going to make a big deal out of it.

'Yes,' said Finn, sounding almost as dazed as she felt. 'I suppose it was.'

'And at least we know we can do it now.'

'Yes.'

An agonising pause. What should she do now? Kate wondered wildly. Reassure him that it wouldn't happen again? Ignore the whole thing? Or finish putting the plates away?

In the end it was Finn who broke the silence. 'I've got a few letters to write,' he said as if he had never kissed her, never had his fingers entwined in her hair. 'I'll be in my study if you need me.'

Kate watched him go, churning with frustration and still dizzy with desire. Perhaps she should go along in a few minutes and knock on his study door and tell him that she needed him to take her upstairs and make love to her all night and promise to let her stay with him for ever.

She wouldn't, of course. She wasn't supposed to need him for anything more intimate than the need to service the boiler, or to sort out a muddle with her housekeeping money.

Drearily, Kate picked up the plates once more. Thinking about that look on Finn's face after he had kissed her made her wince. The kiss had been a mistake.

It hadn't felt like a mistake, though. Not to her.

But Finn clearly wished it had never happened. She should never have suggested it, Kate realised. They had just got to the stage where they could talk to each other without too much constraint, and now the kiss had changed everything. Finn had retreated to his study, and there was no point in hoping that he would emerge ready to discuss what had happened. Kate was prepared to bet that he had never read any of those magazine articles which insisted on the importance of communication and talking things through in a successful relationship.

Not that they *had* a relationship, she reminded herself with a sigh. She had a job, and Finn had a potential embarrassment, but that wasn't much of a basis on which to build a life together, was it?

It didn't stop her waiting tensely for Finn to make at least some reference to the fact that they had kissed. It had been pretty shattering, after all, and judging from his expression when he let her go, for him as well as for her.

But Finn never so much as mentioned it. He carried on exactly as before, having apparently wiped the whole experience from his mind. Kate wished, not without some resentment, that she could do the same, but the memory of that devastating kiss was like a constant strumming just beneath her skin, leaving her edgy and unable to settle.

The days weren't too bad, and there were times when she was walking Derek or laughing with Alex that Kate even managed to persuade herself that she was well on the way to forgetting it quite as effectively as Finn. And then he would come back from work and walk into the kitchen looking solid and austere, and she would remember the kiss in such vivid detail that he might as well have bent her over the kitchen table and kissed her all over again.

Although *that* clearly wasn't going to happen. Finn was polite but guarded, and he was very careful to keep his distance. Even a brush of the fingers was clearly out. Swinging wildly between resentment and frustration, Kate grew increasingly tetchy with him until even Finn was driven to comment.

'What's the matter with you at the moment?'

'Nothing.'

'Please don't make me guess,' he said with an exasperated sigh. 'I've had a difficult day and I'm not in the mood for playing games. You might as well just tell me what's wrong.'

Oh, yes, she could just see herself doing that! Well, Finn, she could say, the thing is that I'm desperately in love with you and finding it all a bit frustrating. I know you'd rather pick up slugs, but do you think you could just take me to bed anyway and make me feel better?

Kate was half tempted to say it just to provoke Finn into a reaction other than his habitual range from expressionless to irritable but, as she strongly suspected that it would turn out to be one of unadulterated horror, she thought she would spare herself the humiliation. She took out her feelings on the potatoes instead, mashing them with a vengeance.

'There's nothing wrong,' she said. 'What could be wrong? I'm just doing my job.'

Finn wrenched off his tie and tossed it onto the back of a chair. 'Your job doesn't involve you carrying on like an aggrieved wife!'

'No,' Kate agreed, banging the potato masher onto the side of the saucepan with unnecessary force. 'It involves looking after you, your daughter, your house and your dog. I don't have time to behave like a wife, let alone an aggrieved one!'

He sighed irritably. 'If you want some time off, Kate, why don't you just tell me?'

'Look, I'm just in a bad mood, all right?' she snapped. If he pushed her any further she jolly well *would* tell him what was bothering her, and then he'd be sorry! 'There doesn't have to be a reason, does there? Or is there a clause in my contract which says I have to be Mary Poppins the whole time?'

'If this is just a bad mood, perhaps you'd better have the night off anyway,' said Finn.

'It's a bit late for that now,' Kate pointed out crossly. 'Besides, I'm going out tomorrow night.'

'Oh? Who with?' he demanded, sounding oddly disgruntled for a man who only a moment ago had been practically pushing her out of the door.

'With you,' said Kate. 'We're having drinks with your neighbour.'

The dark brows drew together ominously. 'Which neighbour?' he asked with foreboding.

'Laura. She's been away for a few weeks and thought it would be nice to catch up on all your news.'

Laura had been a very glamorous divorcee, and Kate had identified a distinctly predatory gleam in her eyes when she had rung the bell earlier that evening and asked for Finn. She hadn't been at all pleased to see Kate instead of Rosa, and even less happy when Kate made sure she could see the engagement ring on her finger.

Finn was still scowling. 'I hope you said I was busy.'

'No, I said we'd love to come.'

'We?'

'Yes, *we*, you and me! I realise that you've wiped it from your mind, but we are supposed to be engaged!'

'Pretending to be engaged!'

Kate flushed. 'That's what I meant.'

'And it's only when Stella's here,' Finn went on crossly. 'There's no need to rope the neighbours into this particular fantasy!'

'I wasn't roping anyone in,' she protested. 'This woman came to the door, clearly planning an intimate tête-à-tête with you while I had this whacking great ring on my finger. Of course she noticed it straight away, that's what women do.' No need to tell Finn that she had made quite sure that Laura had seen it and was forced to comment on it. 'What was I supposed to do? Pretend I didn't exist?'

'You could have said you were engaged to someone else.'

'Oh, well, excuse me while I just go and shoot myself,' said Kate sarcastically. 'I am just so useless at telepathy and knowing who I'm allowed to tell and who I'm not! What's the big problem with Laura knowing anyway?' she added as a sudden suspicion crossed her mind.

Finn was pouring himself a large whisky. 'The problem is that I've been avoiding that woman ever since she moved in next door and discovered that I was a widower. I've managed to fob her off so far by saying that I'm not ready for another relationship.'

'So? Tell her that you changed your mind when you met me.'

Dream on, Kate!

'Great! So when you go, I'll have to tell her that our ''engagement'' is off, and then she'll think there's no reason for me not to think about another relationship,' grumbled Finn.

'You'll just have to learn to say no rather than hiding behind the fact that you're a widower,' said Kate robustly. 'I wouldn't have thought *you* would find that too hard,' she added with a slight edge. 'Off-putting seems to be your speciality!'

He paused with his glass halfway to his lips. 'What do you mean by that?'

'Well, you're not exactly approachable, are you?' she said, putting on oven gloves. 'This Laura must be a brave woman or very thick-skinned if she's been after you all that time. The rest of us wouldn't dare—we're all terrified of you!'

'I can't say I've ever noticed you being very terrified,' said Finn with an acid look.

'I just put a good face on it,' said Kate. 'I told you I was good at acting'

'You must be even better than I thought,' he said dryly, and for some reason the kitchen flared suddenly with the memory of the kiss they had shared. It burned in the air between them, bright and dangerous and so vivid that Kate could practically see herself clinging to him, practically feel his lips, and his hands in her hair.

Jerking her eyes away, she bent to take the casserole out of the oven, glad of the excuse to hide her hot face. 'Maybe I am,' she said, not quite as steadily as she would have liked.

By the time she straightened and had taken off the lid to stir, Finn was sitting at the table, staring broodingly down into his whisky.

'You didn't really say we would go round for drinks tomorrow, did you?'

'Yes, I did.' Kate had herself back under control. 'I didn't see any reason not to,' she said, sniffing appreciatively at the casserole. 'Once Laura discovered that she couldn't have you to herself, she started talking about inviting other people as well. It might be fun.'

Finn grunted. 'Making polite chit-chat over a lukewarm drink doesn't sound like much fun to me!'

'Oh, come on, you might meet someone interesting.'

'And what about Alex?' he said as if she hadn't spoken.

Kate rolled her eyes as she turned from the cooker. 'We're only going next door for an hour or so. Alex could probably come with us, or I'll ask Bella or Phoebe to come over. I'm sure they wouldn't mind. Anyway, I've accepted for you, so you'll have to go now,' she said putting an end to the argument. She started to untie her apron. 'See if you can get home a bit earlier tomorrow evening—we're invited for half past six.'

*　　*　　*

'You look nice.' Bella was playing cards with Alex at the kitchen table when Kate came downstairs the next evening wearing a full skirt with a tight waist and a laced top. 'Very Nell Gwynn! All the men will be panting to buy oranges from you!'

Kate tugged fretfully at her neckline. 'You don't think this is a bit low?'

'No, if you've got it, flaunt it!' said Bella cheerfully.

'I wish I'd brought more clothes with me. Laura looked awfully sophisticated.'

'I think you look beautiful,' said Alex loyally. 'Don't you, Dad?'

Kate spun round. She hadn't heard Finn come into the kitchen behind her, and her heart jerked at the sight of him, tall and austere in a dark suit.

He looked at Kate. 'She looks fine,' he said.

'Oh, Mr McBride, please stop!' said Kate, hiding her disappointment behind a pretence at being overcome. 'You'll turn my head with all these compliments!'

Finn sighed. 'You look absolutely beautiful...stunning...glamorous... What else am I supposed to say?'

'Thin,' prompted Kate.

'Sexy,' Bella suggested.

His eyes rested on Kate's cleavage. 'And sexy,' he said.

There was a tiny pause. Finn checked his watch. 'If you've quite finished fishing for compliments, we'd better go,' he said brusquely. 'The sooner we get there, the sooner we can leave.'

'Quite the party animal, isn't he?' said Bella.

Kate took him by the arm to turn him towards the door. 'Stop grumbling, it'll be fine,' she said. 'Just think of it as a dry run for when Stella comes—and you might at least *try* to look as if you're happy to be with me!'

As she had suspected, Laura had abandoned the idea of intimate drinks alone with Finn since Kate had thrust a spoke in her wheel, and a number of other neighbours had been invited along as well. The women were all wearing discreetly elegant numbers and Kate knew from the moment Laura opened the door that the laced top had been a mistake. Next to the others, she looked garish and flamboyant and more than a little tarty.

Her outfit seemed to go down very well with their husbands, though. Since it was too late to go for a sophisticated image, Kate opted for being fun instead, and Finn grew more and more boot-faced at the gales of laughter coming from the group around her.

'You're back early,' said Bella when they returned. 'We weren't expecting you back for ages. How did it go?'

'Excellent,' Finn bit out. 'Kate managed to ruin my reputation and break up several of my neighbour's marriages in a few short minutes!'

'I don't know what you're talking about,' said Kate crossly, still flushed and more than a little annoyed at being dragged away from the party on the flimsiest of excuses. She had been quite enjoying herself.

'Oh, yes, you do!' snarled Finn. 'You made a complete exhibition of yourself! Laura won't be at all surprised to hear our ''engagement'' is off after the way you were carrying on,' he said furiously. 'You were practically in Tom Anderson's lap!'

'I was not! Not that you would have been able to notice even if I had been,' she retorted. 'You spent the entire time pinned in the corner by Laura and you weren't exactly struggling to get free and circulate. Your body language is very revealing you know.'

'Not as revealing as that top,' Finn snapped back.

'Now, now, children, play nicely,' said Bella. 'I think you'd better work on how to look as if you're engaged before Stella arrives,' she told them. 'You see, generally when people get engaged it's because they love each other and want to spend the rest of their lives together, and not because they fight at parties. That usually comes *after* they get married!' she explained kindly.

'We're certainly going to have to do something different when Stella gets here,' said Finn. 'She's never going to believe we're a couple if Kate carries on the way she did this evening!'

'That shouldn't be a problem,' Kate informed him loftily. 'I was just excited at being appreciated for a change, and I know that's not going to happen when I'm with you!'

'Perhaps you need to give Stella a bit more evidence,' Bella put in diplomatically. 'I was talking to Phoebe while you were out, and we thought it would be a good idea to have a sort of engagement party for you while Stella's here. It's the sort of thing we would do if you were really engaged, and as you're a friend of Gib's, Finn, and Kate's a friend of Phoebe's, it would be natural for them to have a dinner for you and close friends—that's me and Josh and partners.'

She turned her blue gaze on Finn. 'We'll invite your sister along, of course. I'm sure if she saw your friends treating you as an engaged couple she'd be quite convinced, no matter how much you and Kate seemed to argue.'

'It's possible,' said Finn grudgingly, still in a bad mood with Kate. 'But there's no need for you to go to any trouble. This whole business is getting out of control as it is, without you and Phoebe getting involved as well.'

'Don't worry about us,' said Bella. 'Any excuse for a party! What do you think, Kate?'

Kate suspected, like Finn, that things could easily get out of control, but he had been so irritating this evening that she didn't feel like supporting him now. 'I think it's a wonderful idea,' she said firmly. 'I'll give Phoebe a ring tomorrow and we'll sort out a date.'

Stella was due to arrive the following Tuesday. Kate spent the day before spring-cleaning the house from top to bottom. She put flowers in the guest room and set out soap and towels before shutting the door so that Derek couldn't roll on the bed. This was a new trick of his that worked better, from a canine point of view at least, the wetter and muddier he was. It hadn't gone down at all well with Finn when Derek had tried it on his bed.

She had planned a special welcome dinner for Stella, too, and was making individual rich chocolate mousses when Finn came down from saying goodnight to Alex the night before she was due to arrive.

'Is everything under control?'

'I think so,' said Kate. After that disastrous evening at Laura's, they had both recovered their equilibrium and were being polite to each other with only the occasional sharp aside. 'I've just got to finish these now. Her room is ready for her, and I'll put some champagne in the fridge tomorrow.'

Finn raised his brows. 'Champagne?'

'It's a celebration,' she pointed out with an edge of exasperation. 'You haven't seen your sister for a while, and we're getting married— at least as far as she's concerned. Of course we've got to have champagne!'

'If you say so.' Finn dipped his finger into the chocolate mixture, just managing to whip it out of the bowl before Kate swiped it.

'There's no point in going through with the whole pretence unless we're going to do it properly,' she said.

'No, you're right.' He licked his finger, ignoring her frown. 'This chocolate stuff is good.'

Carefully, Kate poured the chocolate mixture into individual ramekins. She waited until she had divided the last of it before asking Finn the question that was most on her mind. 'Do you think we'll be able to carry it off?'

'If we don't lose our nerve. Stella's very astute, though, so we can't afford to relax while she's here. She'll pick up instantly on anything odd. In fact—'

'What?' asked Kate when he stopped abruptly.

Finn didn't answer immediately. He paced around the table, his hands in his pockets and his shoulders hunched, debating whether to continue or not.

'I'm not sure how to ask you this, Kate,' he said at last, 'but I wonder how you would feel about sleeping with me while Stella is here.' He saw Kate's head jerk up from the bowl she was scraping and corrected himself hurriedly. 'I don't mean *sleep* with me, of course,' he said. 'I just mean…share a room.'

Of course. He wouldn't want to sleep with her, would he? Kate put down the bowl.

'I think Stella would think it a bit strange if we didn't,' Finn went on.

It's not a big deal. Wasn't that what she had said to Bella? She was the girl who wasn't going to take the situation seriously. The actress who wasn't bothered by silly little things like kisses or jumping into bed with her boss. She couldn't change her image now.

Kate started gathering up whisks and spoons and bowls to wash. 'Sure,' she said.

Finn looked at her, taken aback by her ready agreement. 'You will?'

'I was just saying that we might as well do the thing properly,' she pointed out reasonably. 'I don't mind sharing with you while your sister is around. I know you wouldn't...' She trailed off, embarrassed when it came to the crunch. 'That we wouldn't...you know...'

'I know,' he said dryly.

'We might as well start tonight, don't you think?' Kate suggested, determined to recover her confidence and carry the situation off with style. 'Then we'll look more natural when she gets here tomorrow morning.'

Of course, it was all very well being brisk and practical in the kitchen, but it was a different matter when the moment came. At least she had a nightdress with her. Kate got undressed in her own room and put it on, smoothing the silky material over her hips. She couldn't believe that she was actually going to walk along to Finn's bedroom and get into bed beside him! Her whole body was pumping and twitching with nerves.

Not a big deal, right?

Right.

Wrapping a dressing gown tightly around her, Kate took a deep breath and opened her door.

Finn was waiting for her, looking ill at ease in a crumpled pair of pyjamas. Kate guessed that he didn't normally wear them and had dug them out of a drawer to preserve the decencies.

'I'll take a pillow and sleep on the floor,' he said when she hesitated in the doorway.

'That defeats the purpose of the exercise, doesn't it?' Kate was amazed at how cool she sounded. 'What if Stella came in and saw that you were sleeping down there? It looks like a big bed,' she went on, still without a tremor, and she even managed a sort of laugh. 'I trust you to keep your hands off me!'

A wary expression had descended on Finn's face. He was probably baffled by her transformation from messy, muddled sentimentality to brisk practicality.

'Which side do you normally sleep?' said Kate, taking matters into her own hands.

'Over here.' He pointed, and she walked round the bed to the other side and pulled back the duvet. Taking off her dressing gown, she draped it over a chair and got into bed. If Finn was waiting for her to make a fuss about the situation, he would have a long wait. Bella would be proud of her. She was cool.

After another puzzled glance, Finn switched off the main light. Kate pretended to be making herself comfortable as the bed creaked and dipped when he got in the other side and clicked off the bedside lamp.

'Well…goodnight,' he said.

'Goodnight.'

There, that was easy, thought Kate, trying not to think about the fact that Finn was lying bare inches away, or about how easy it would be to roll against him in the night. He flexed his shoulders to make himself comfortable and she caught her breath, wondering if it might just be the prelude to him moving closer…but no. He settled and lay still, and after a while there was only the steady sound of him breathing quietly in the dark.

Very, very gradually, Kate let herself relax. When it was obvious that Finn had fallen asleep, she congratulated herself on her cool. Really, there was nothing to it. Everything would be fine.

CHAPTER NINE

It was still dark when Kate drifted out of sleep to find herself lying on her side with an arm over her. A hard, male arm holding her against the hard, male body behind her.

Finn. He must have rolled over in his sleep, she realised, blinking dreamily. She could feel his breath, deep and slow, just stirring her hair and that was enough to wake every nerve in her body, and set each one tingling, alert with wicked anticipation. 'No going back to sleep now!' they seemed to scoff at Kate's attempts to close her mind to his closeness. 'It's too late for that.'

It was much too late. Even with her eyes squeezed shut, Kate was aware of every millimetre of her own body, burning where it touched his. It felt so good to be held by him. She wished she could turn and nuzzle in to him, to wake him with soft kisses, and her eyes snapped open as her entrails liquefied at the thought.

She *could* turn.

She could kiss him.

She could pretend that she was sleeping too.

Once the idea was in her head, she couldn't dislodge it. It would be silly, and it might be very embarrassing, the sensible part of Kate's mind pointed out. She was supposed to be keeping her distance and impressing him with her cool. Snuggling up against him and running her hands over his body while she kissed her way to his mouth wouldn't do that.

But it would feel so good.

She could always stop, Kate reasoned to herself. She didn't have to go that far. She didn't even need to wake him. She just wanted a glimpse of what it would be like if she belonged here in his arms, if Finn knew exactly who he was holding against him and would smile at the feel of her lips on his skin.

That wasn't asking too much, was it?

Kate stirred experimentally, but Finn just kept breathing into her hair. He must be sound asleep, she thought with a spurt of resentment. How could he be sleeping when she was awake and churning with desire? Couldn't he feel how much she wanted him?

Well, she could lie here all night or she could see what would happen if she turned over. She might as well accept that she wasn't going to go back to sleep either way.

Taking a deep breath, she sighed as if she were dreaming and rolled towards Finn, who promptly rolled away in his turn to lie on his back, the arm that had been around her now outflung across the pillow.

Typical. Kate eyed his slumbering form with frustration. Even in sleep he seemed determined to resist her. Well, they would see about *that*!

She shifted across the sheet, warm from his body, until she could snuggle into the solid strength of him. Finn was much taller than her standing up, but lying down Kate just fitted him nicely. She was very comfortable pressed into his side. She could put an arm over his chest to keep him close and rest her face against his throat, breathing in the scent of his skin, and all without him waking.

Stop now, Kate told herself sternly. Comfort wasn't everything, but it was enough for now.

Only it wasn't. Of course it wasn't.

Without making a conscious decision, Kate touched her lips to Finn's throat, and then again, and again, until she was working her way up and along his jaw. Her hand seemed to have acquired a will of its own, too, sliding under the pyjama jacket and around his lean waist.

She was playing with fire, and she knew it, but she couldn't help herself and she didn't care. Her kisses drifted back down to his collar, and she was just unfastening the top button when all at once Finn's breathing stilled.

She had woken him. Slowly, Kate lifted her head until she could look down into his face and see the gleam of his eyes in the darkness. She couldn't pretend that she was asleep now. With one part of her mind she registered that she might regret this moment in the morning, but now…oh, now was not the time for regrets.

Finn lay motionless beneath her, blinking away sleep. Kate could see him trying to adjust to wakefulness, and she braced herself for the moment when he realised who she was and what she was doing and jackknifed away from her in horror. But he just stared up at her for a long, long time before the arm behind her head came round so that his fingers could slide into her hair, and pull her head down towards him with exquisite, dreamlike slowness.

When their lips met at last, the dreaminess shattered and Kate sank into Finn and they kissed hungrily, again and again, as if to make up for all the waiting. Finn's other hand was sliding insistently over her satin nightdress, searching for the hem, and when he found it, it slipped beneath, rucking up the slithery material as he explored her thigh, the back of her knee, the curve of her hip.

The feel of his hand on her bare skin made Kate gasp, and fumble for the buttons of his pyjama jacket, but her fingers were so clumsy that in the end Finn simply pulled it over his head before rolling her beneath him abruptly. With a sigh of release, Kate wound her arms around his neck, pulling him closer, luxuriating in the feel of his bare back under her hands.

She was terrified that Finn would wake properly and realise what he was doing. She didn't care about the morning, didn't think about what they would do and say to explain this away. For now all Kate wanted was to abandon herself completely, to the touch of his hands, to the feel of his mouth as it drifted tantalisingly over her, to the hard demand of his body.

To the clutching pleasure and the slow, irresistible burn of excitement that left them gasping and powerless while a timeless rhythm swept them both up, up, up, too high, beyond thought, beyond feeling, to the very edge until

Kate fell abruptly, tumbling into a heart-stopping intensity of sensation.

When she came to, Finn was lying heavily on top of her, breathing raggedly. She was having trouble working her lungs herself. They seemed to have forgotten how to function by themselves, and it took a conscious effort to draw each tiny, shuddering breath.

After a while, Finn moved away from her, muttering something that Alex would have had no trouble in identifying as a rude word.

Oh, yes! Kate wanted to say. Yes, indeed! But she thought she had better not.

He lay on his back beside her, trying to bring his breathing under control. 'I'm sorry,' he said at last. 'I didn't mean that to happen.'

'It was my fault.' Kate made a half-hearted effort to force some contrition into her voice. She knew she ought to feel guilty, but it was as if all those nerve endings that had been twitching and fretting uncomfortably for the past few weeks were now stretching and smirking with satisfaction. Her body didn't feel guilty at all. It felt very, very good. Better than it ever had before, in fact.

'I forgot where I was.' Which wasn't strictly true, but she was feeling too pleased with herself to worry about little details. 'I suppose I got a bit carried away.'

'I think we both did,' said Finn dryly.

Kate shifted onto her side so that she could look at him properly. 'Are you really sorry?' she made herself ask.

He turned his head on the pillow. 'No,' he said honestly after a moment. 'No, and I can't say that I didn't know what I was doing either, but it was very irresponsible. I wasn't planning on this happening. What if you got pregnant?'

'I won't do that. I'm still on the Pill.'

She still felt amazing, relaxed and replete. Even her toes were tingling with remembered pleasure. It wasn't a feeling she wanted to give up, not yet anyway. Given half a chance, she knew that Finn would say that it should never happen again. Kate wasn't sure that she could bear that.

'Look,' she said persuasively, 'we haven't hurt anybody else tonight. I think we both needed a bit of comfort, and we took it. What's wrong with that?'

She would have to be careful not to alarm Finn by seeming too keen. 'It doesn't mean anything to either of us,' she told him, 'but that's no reason why we shouldn't have some fun. It's not as if we're talking about for ever.

I'm only here for a few weeks, and since we're going to be sharing a room, don't you think we should make the most of it? Unless you'd rather not,' she finished lamely, unnerved by the way Finn was watching her in silence.

'I daresay I could resign myself to it,' he said.

It took a few moments for Kate to realise that he was teasing. Dizzy with relief, she smiled at him. 'It would only be a temporary thing,' she tried to reassure him. 'Just while your sister is here.'

'Of course,' said Finn expressionlessly.

'No big deal.'

'No.'

'Neither of us is going to get involved.'

'Right.'

Silence. Kate studied Finn a little uneasily, not sure what to make of his curt replies. Was he regretting his decision already? In the darkness, his face was even harder to read than usual.

The main thing was that he hadn't repulsed her, she reasoned. There would be more nights like this. She couldn't ask for more than that. It was greedy to want him to love her as well, to want her for ever.

For now, Kate decided, she would do what she had said she would do, and make the most of what she had. She looked at Finn through the darkness and thought about his lips against her skin and the feel of his body beneath her hands, and the breath dried in her throat. For now, that was enough.

'Anyway, I'm sorry if I woke you,' she said, and then shivered with pleasure as Finn reached out and pulled her unresisting towards him.

'How sorry?' he asked.

She smiled as he kissed her. 'I'll show you,' she said.

The crunch of tyres on the gravel drive sent Derek into a frenzy of barking, and Kate paused in front of the hall mirror, running her fingers through her hair in a vain attempt to smooth her wild curls. She was surprisingly nervous about meeting Stella. Finn and Alex had gone to pick her up from the airport, and now this would be the moment of truth.

In the cool light of morning, Finn had made no reference to the night before. He had behaved so exactly as normal, grumbling about the state of the kitchen and refusing to allow Alex to meet her aunt in combat trousers and scruffy trainers, that Kate might have wondered if it had just been a wonderful dream if her body wasn't still pulsing with remembered pleasure.

Reeling, replete and short of sleep, she could hardly string two words together, and her conversation at breakfast had been completely incoherent, at least judging by the funny looks Alex had given her. It was just lucky that Finn had to do the driving and not her.

Now she had to face the terrifyingly astute and perceptive Stella. Still, thought Kate with one last glance at her reflection as she headed for the door, there shouldn't be any problem convincing Stella that *she* was in love. She had that dazed, dopey look down pat.

On first sight, Stella had little in common with her brother. Several years older than Finn, she was plump and elegant, with beautifully cut grey hair, but she had the same shrewd grey eyes.

Waiting to greet her on the doorstep, Kate found herself enveloped in a warm hug. 'I cannot *tell* you how glad I am that Finn has found someone at last!' said Stella. She held Kate at arms' length and examined her face. 'Finn didn't tell me how pretty you were.'

Didn't he think she was pretty? Kate wondered with a pang. What *had* he told Stella, exactly? That she was nice-enough looking, but could never compare to the exquisite Isabel?

Finn was lifting an enormous suitcase out of the car. 'She's not pretty,' he said to his sister, whose jaw dropped, and even Kate was taken aback. She wasn't that bad, was she?

She stuck on a smile. Luckily, some people hadn't forgotten that they were supposed to be engaged! 'Thanks!' she said, finding no trouble at all in acting the part of aggrieved fiancée right then. 'You know, there's such a thing as being *too* honest!'

He set the suitcase on the gravel. 'I don't think you are pretty,' he said. 'Pretty's not enough for you.' He glanced at his sister, who was looking indignant on Kate's behalf. 'She's beautiful, not pretty,' he said, 'and I didn't tell you because I thought you'd be able to see it for yourself.'

There was a moment of stunned silence. Kate's face was hot and she stood feeling foolish and unsure what to do with herself. Finn had sounded so convincing that for a second or two there she had even wondered if he meant it. He was a better actor than she had thought.

Stella recovered first. 'Isn't that typical of Finn?' she said, linking arms with Kate. 'He gets you really cross and then says something like that which makes it impossible to stay furious the way you want to, so he always gets the last word!'

Alex was desperate to introduce her aunt to Derek, who was scratching behind the door to be let out to join the excitement, but the meeting was not a huge success. Stella was unimpressed.

'What kind of dog is *that*?'

'A very badly behaved one,' said Finn.

Alex leapt to Derek's defence. 'He's not!' she said hotly. 'He's very intelligent and perfectly trained, isn't he, Kate?'

'Well, maybe not *perfectly*,' Kate amended, thinking of the hours she had spent chasing Derek to try and get him on the lead, not to mention the chewed shoes and the stolen meat and the bed-rolling game.

Stella eyed Derek askance. She didn't actually say that he was the ugliest dog that she had ever seen, but she might as well have done. 'Where on earth did you find him?'

'It's Kate's fault,' said Finn. 'She fell into a pile of rubbish and came up with the dog, who has single-pawedly managed to disrupt my home and my office and is now costing me a fortune in vet bills and dog food!'

'Oh, Dad…!' said Alex reproachfully, and he smiled as he put an arm around her and hugged her.

Stella's eyes narrowed speculatively as she studied first her brother and her niece, and then Kate. 'It looks like things have changed around here,' she said.

Apparently it wasn't just her brother who had changed. She frowned in a way that reminded Kate of Finn as she looked around the kitchen. 'I can't quite put my finger on it, but the whole house seems different,' she said. 'It's much warmer and more inviting somehow.'

Kate tried to see the room through a stranger's eyes. Already the kitchen seemed utterly familiar to her, although it wasn't quite as pristine as when she had first seen it, it had to be admitted. 'I think Finn would tell you it's much messier,' she said ruefully.

'I certainly would,' he said, getting mugs out of the cupboard. 'We can blame Kate for the difference in the house too.'

'Well, I think it's a great improvement,' said Stella as Kate plunged the cafetière.

Finn put the mugs on the table. 'So do I,' he said.

Kate's breath clogged in her throat. 'I'll remember that the next time you complain about my mess,' she managed, not knowing what to do except make a joke out of it, as the alternative was to throw her arms around him and beg him to say that he meant it. 'Alex, you're my witness!'

Stella was obviously dying for a chance to get Kate on her own, so she waved aside Finn's offer to show her to her room. 'You come with me, Kate,' she said.

Upstairs, she looked around the guest bedroom with pleasure. 'It all looks perfectly lovely,' she said, sniffing one of the scented soaps that Kate had put out for her. 'You're spoiling me—thank you!'

Kate shifted uncomfortably. 'I know Finn appreciates you coming all this way,' she said. 'He's told me how much you've done for him since Isabel died.'

'Oh, that was a terrible time,' sighed Stella, sinking down onto the bed. 'I did what I could, but Finn isn't easy to help. He keeps things to himself too much. Well, you must know how stubborn he is! It broke my heart to see him struggle on his own all these years. Sometimes it seemed as if he wouldn't ever let himself be happy again.'

'He loved Isabel very much.' Kate made herself say Isabel's name. It was as well to remember that last night didn't change anything, and that whatever Finn might say in front of his sister, her place in his life was only ever going to be temporary.

'I know he did,' said Stella, 'but he had Alex to think of as well as himself. I've been telling him for years that she needed a mother figure, and look at the difference in her now! I've never seen her so animated. She's come out of herself completely, and Finn says it's all thanks to you.'

She smiled at Kate. 'What he doesn't realise, of course, being a man, is that the real difference is in *him*. For years it's been like he was holed up behind a brick wall, refusing to let anyone close, but you've got under his guard. You must have done if you got him to give a home to that funny little dog! Finn doesn't even like dogs.'

'I think he likes Derek more than he admits,' said Kate loyally.

'That just proves my point!' said Stella getting to her feet. 'I haven't seen him look this happy and relaxed for years, and it's all because of you.' There were tears in her eyes as she embraced Kate. 'Finn won't say it, of course—you know what he's like!—but I can tell by the way he looks at you how much he loves you.'

So much for Stella and her famously astute perception!

Kate knew that Finn's sister was wrong. He didn't love her, but he *was* more relaxed, she could see that. Whether he was happy or not, she didn't ask. After Stella's arrival they were rarely alone together except for when they closed the bedroom door at night and they didn't talk then. They had said everything there was to be said that first night.

For both of them, the days that followed were a time out of time. Kate had to keep reminding herself that this was just a brief fling. It was about now and not for ever. They were being grown-up about the whole thing, and not taking it seriously at all. She was in thrall to the long, sweet nights they spent together, and refused to spoil them by thinking about the future or reminding Finn of reality. There would be time enough for that when Stella went home to Canada.

That was what Kate told herself, but it didn't stop her falling deeper and deeper in love with him. Sometimes she would look at him being perfectly ordinary like driving or putting on his glasses to read the paper, or just sitting and listening to his sister and daughter, and the air would evaporate from her lungs, while her heart clutched with the need to go over and touch him, to press her lips to his skin, and wind her arms around his neck and whisper a plea for him to take her upstairs, *now*.

Stella was a demanding guest, but Kate liked her much more than she had expected to. She was forthright and brisk at times, and she could be very tactless with Alex, but she clearly adored Finn, and she entered into whatever was going on with boundless enthusiasm. When Kate broached the idea of going to an engagement party at Phoebe's, Stella was thrilled.

'That sounds like a wonderful idea!' she said. 'If you hadn't been so obviously in love, I might be wondering if you two were actually going to get married,' she said that night over supper. 'You don't seem to be making any plans. Have you even picked a date for the wedding?'

Finn glanced at Kate. 'There isn't any rush.'

'There isn't any reason to wait, either,' Stella pointed out tartly. 'You're both old enough to know your own minds, neither of you has any other commitments and you're even living together. What's wrong with going ahead and getting married?'

'That's between Kate and I,' said Finn, gritting his teeth at his sister's interference.

'Of course, but you might think about other people, too.' Stella wasn't ready to give up yet. 'If you give us enough warning, Geoff and the kids can come over with me. I'm sure Kate's parents will want to know when the wedding is going to be too.'

'They're away at the moment,' said Kate, seizing on the excuse. 'That's one of the reasons we're waiting. I haven't told them about Finn yet.'

'Well, I don't see the need for all this secrecy,' grumbled Stella. 'Thank goodness these friends of yours are prepared to get into the right spirit and have a bit of a celebration! If it was left to you two it might never happen.'

'Stella, will you please stop trying to organise our lives? Kate and I are perfectly happy.'

'If you're not going to think about your-selves, you might at least think about Alex.'

'Alex is perfectly happy with the way things are, too,' said Finn tensely. 'Aren't you, Alex?'

'Ye-es,' Alex agreed cautiously. 'But it would be better if you and Kate did get married,' she added, taking Finn and Kate aback. 'Then I'd know Kate would stay for ever and look after Derek.'

Stella shot her brother a triumphant look. 'Your daughter's got more sense than you,' she told him. 'I might not make that dog my priority, but in every other way she's got it right. You'll lose Kate if you're not careful, and you don't want that, do you?'

Finn looked across the table at Kate, who was looking acutely uncomfortable. She was wearing one of those vibrantly coloured tops of hers and her hair tumbled as messily as ever to her shoulders. Her cheeks were flushed, and the brown eyes which met his for a fleeting moment were bright and clear.

'No,' he agreed softly, 'I don't want that.'

'Hey!' Kate thought it was time to lighten the atmosphere. 'I'm not going anywhere. This is a very nice house and Derek is a very nice dog, and I suppose you two aren't bad either,' she added, winking at Alex. 'Why wouldn't I stay for ever?'

To her surprise, Alex came to stand by her side 'Do you promise?' she said intensely.

What could she say? Kate put an arm around her to hug her close. 'I promise,' she said, and wished that it could be true.

'It's going to be a posh-frock affair,' Phoebe told Kate on the phone the next day. 'Make sure you all come dressed up to the nines.'

'Bella said it was just supper.'

'No, we've decided to have a proper dinner party since you and Finn met at dinner here.'

Kate held the phone away from her ear and stared at it in a puzzled manner. 'We met at work, Phoebe!'

'You met here for the first time socially,' said Phoebe firmly. 'And we want to make it a proper celebration for you.'

'Phoebe,' said Kate carefully, lowering her voice in case Stella came into the kitchen. 'You do know that Finn and I aren't really engaged, don't you? The party is just a bit of icing on the cake to convince his sister.'

'Of course I remember,' said Phoebe with such dignity that Kate was pretty sure that she and Bella had got carried away with their planning and forgotten little details like the fact that she and Finn weren't actually going to get married at all. 'But that's no reason not to do things in style,' she added, making a swift recovery.

'Well, don't get carried away!'

Phoebe pretended to sound hurt. 'Would I?'

'Bella would,' said Kate. 'Keep her under control, Phoebs. Stella seems to have accepted our supposed engagement so far, but she's not an idiot and she's bound to get suspicious if you go over-the-top with this dinner.'

'Relax,' said Phoebe soothingly. 'It'll be fun!'

Kate wasn't so sure. She loved her friends dearly, but she was ridiculously nervous about the night ahead as she and Finn got ready to go out that evening. It was hard enough keeping up the pretence in front of Stella without the interested gaze of all her closest friends on her. They would be watching her and Finn together and, knowing Phoebe and Bella, it wouldn't take them any time to see how she really felt about him. Kate just hoped they wouldn't give her away.

'I wish we weren't going out,' she sighed as she searched for her favourite earrings on top of the chest of drawers.

In the mirror above, she could see Finn shrugging himself into a shirt. The casual intimacy of getting dressed in the same room still gave Kate a tiny thrill each time.

'I know,' he said as he began fastening buttons. 'I'd rather stay in myself, but Stella is raring to meet everyone else.' He sighed. 'She's probably hoping to recruit some allies in her campaign for an early wedding.'

'It's all getting a bit complicated, isn't it?' said Kate, thinking of the promise she had made to Alex. She shouldn't have made a promise she couldn't keep, she thought guiltily.

'It's my fault,' said Finn. He tucked his shirt into his trousers. 'I should have known that my sister wouldn't stop at satisfying herself that you really existed. She won't be happy until she has the details of table settings and flowers and which hymns we have chosen!' He reached for a tie and looped it round his neck. 'I tell you, sometimes I wish we had never started this pretence!'

'Do you?' asked Kate.

Finn's hand stilled at his tie and his eyes met hers in the mirror. 'No,' he said.

His cool grey gaze locked with her warm brown one in the mirror, and for Kate it was as if the world stopped turning. Without taking his eyes from hers, Finn finished his tie and walked over slowly to put his hands on her shoulders.

'I can't imagine what we did without you,' he said as if coming into the middle of a conversation. 'Whenever Stella has been over before the visits have been a bit tense, but it's gone really well this time, and it's all due to you. Stella thinks you're wonderful.'

He paused, his hands warm and strong on her shoulders, and Kate let herself lean back against him just because she could and it felt so good.

'I've never thanked you properly for everything you've done,' Finn said soberly. 'And I don't just mean the pretence. The house looks great, you produce endless good meals, and then there's Alex...she's happy.'

'And you?' Kate nerved herself to ask.

Finn turned her slowly between his hands until she was facing him and he could look down into her face. 'I'm happy, too,' he said, and bent his head to kiss her.

Kate put her arms around his waist and leant blissfully into him. It wasn't a long kiss, but it was very sweet, and it was the first time he had kissed her when it wasn't dark and there wasn't anyone to convince. This kiss was just between the two of them. Neither of them could pretend now that it was only for show.

'Hey, you guys!' Stella was banging on the door, startling them apart. 'Hurry up, the taxi's here!'

When Finn released her, Kate could barely stand. Adrift in a wash of sensation, she felt oddly insubstantial, as if it was another person entirely who shimmered as she walked down the stairs, got into a taxi, and gave the driver directions to Phoebe's house dropping off Alex with Finn's neighbour first.

'Kate, you look absolutely fabulous!' said Gib, jaw dropping in surprise as he opened the door, and the others were just as complimentary.

'Look at her, she's glowing!'

'It must be love!'

Kate hardly heard any of it. She was finding it hard to concentrate on anything except the thought of going home with Finn, saying good-night to Stella, and closing the bedroom door, when Finn would kiss her again and peel the dress from her shoulders and pull her down onto the wide bed...

'Kate, Kate, wake up!' Bella was waving a hand in front of her face, startling Kate out of her dreams.

'What?'

'We're about to open a bottle of champagne for you. You might at least make an effort to look as if you're on the same planet as the rest of us!'

Blinking, Kate looked around her. Stella was nose to nose with Phoebe and Josh, and the others were encouraging Gib as he eased the cork out of the champagne bottle. Finn was there, too, but slightly apart, smiling austerely, and Kate felt herself melting inside as someone put a glass of champagne into her hand.

'OK,' said Gib, when the champagne had been poured and everyone had a glass. 'I'd like to propose a toast to Finn and Kate. Unlikely as it seemed at first, they seem to go together perfectly, and I think we all want to wish them every happiness, because they both deserve it more than anyone else I can think of.'

'To Finn and Kate!' the others chorused. 'Hear, hear!'

Kate looked at Finn, wondering what they were supposed to do now. He didn't seem particularly perturbed, it had to be said. His grey eyes were alight, and he was smiling, and she couldn't help smiling back.

Oblivious to everyone else, he came over to put his arm around her, and pulled her into his side. 'Thank you,' he said simply. 'We're very grateful to all of you,' he said, glancing around, and then he looked down into Kate's face. Her brown eyes were shining. 'Aren't we, Kate?'

'Yes,' she breathed, not knowing what he said, but understanding that he wanted her to agree with him. 'Oh, yes.' But she wasn't thinking about being grateful, she was just thinking about how much she loved him and how she couldn't wait for his arm to tighten around her and his mouth to come down on hers.

When it did, she gave herself up to the sweetness without a thought for their audience, and when Finn finally released her, it was bizarre to hear a splatter of applause.

'I think that answers all our questions,' said Gib dryly.

'Except when is the wedding?' Stella put in, spotting her chance.

'Yes, good point.' Phoebe and Bella chimed in as Finn released Kate reluctantly. 'When is it?'

Finn didn't take his eyes from Kate's. 'Soon,' he said.

CHAPTER TEN

PHOEBE and Bella had obviously spent days planning and preparing dinner, and had put so much effort into decorating the table and bullying everyone into dressing up that Kate felt desperately guilty that it wasn't for real. They couldn't have made more fuss if she and Finn really had been engaged—in fact, Kate was beginning to suspect that her friends didn't quite believe that the whole thing was a pretence.

Bella's boyfriend, Will, was there, and Josh had brought along a new girlfriend, and together with Phoebe and Gib and Stella, who was on fine form, they made a lively party. Finn and Kate weren't required to contribute much, which was just as well.

Part of Kate wished that she could enjoy it all more, but she was having trouble concentrating on the conversation. All she could think about was going home with Finn and closing the bedroom door and shutting out the rest of the world. She made an effort to laugh and smile at the right points, but with Finn sitting beside her it was hard to focus. She wanted to put her hand on his thigh, to kiss his throat, to make him stand up and drag her away from the chatter and the laughter and the pretending.

'So, that's it then,' said Phoebe, when Kate pulled herself together sufficiently to help carry the plates through to the kitchen after the main course.

'What do you mean?'

'You're in love with Finn, aren't you?'

Kate set the plates carefully on the draining board. 'Why do you say that?'

'It's obvious. I don't think you've even registered that there's anyone else in the room!'

'Sorry,' Kate muttered. 'I really do appreciate all the trouble you and Bella have gone to but...'

'But Finn is the only person in there who seems real?' Phoebe smiled. 'I know.'

'OK, so I am a bit in love with him,' said Kate with a shade of defiance.

'A bit?'

Kate gave in. 'A lot.'

'What about Finn? I mean, I can see he's making an effort to join in, but there's something about the way he's making a point of not looking at you that's a dead give-away. I reckon he's pretty smitten too.'

'I don't think so,' she said sadly. 'He's just a good actor. I haven't told him how I feel, and I'm not going to. We're having a nice time at the moment, but I know it's not going to last. As soon as Stella leaves, I'll get a new job and that will be that. It's just a temporary thing.'

Phoebe looked at Kate in concern. 'Is that going to be enough for you?'

Kate looked bleakly back at her friend. 'It's going to have to be,' she said.

But the conversation with Phoebe had had its effect. It was true that Phoebe knew her better than most, but if her feelings for Finn were that obvious, she would have to be careful.

It would be awful if Finn guessed that she was in love with him. Kate cringed inwardly at the thought. It would make the situation unbearably awkward for them both. The last thing she wanted was to put him in the position of having to explain to her that he wouldn't—couldn't—ever love anyone the same way as he had loved Isabel. It wasn't as if she hadn't known all along that she could never compare to his dead wife.

Kate decided that it would be easier for Finn if she tried to keep more of a distance, but it was hard not to respond when he reached for her in the dark, or to pretend that she wasn't pleased to see him when he walked through the door. She just couldn't do cool and reserved, no matter how hard she tried.

It was even harder when Stella went off to visit various friends. She was away nearly a week, and Kate was alarmed to discover how easy and comfortable it felt with just the three of them—plus the dog, of course—in the house. It was like being a proper family. Sometimes Kate had to make herself remember that she was only a temporary member of it, and that she wouldn't always be able to chatter with Alex or hum as she pottered around the kitchen or climb into bed next to Finn.

Stella's departure should have meant that they could drop the fiction that Kate was more than a housekeeper, but Alex continued to treat her in exactly the same way, and when Finn and Kate discussed the matter in bed the night before she left, they decided that it was hardly worth reverting to the previous sleeping arrangements while she was away.

'You know what Stella's like,' said Finn. 'I wouldn't put it past her to turn up again without warning just to have another nag about fixing a wedding date.'

'We might as well stay as we are, then,' said Kate, trying to sound offhand, as if she didn't really care one way or the other.

'Might as well,' Finn agreed in an equally indifferent voice, but then he rolled Kate beneath him and she felt him smiling as he kissed her throat, and her heart swelled with relief and happiness.

Better to make the most of the time she had left, she decided. Plenty of time to be cool when Stella had gone back to Canada and there was no more reason to share Finn's life, no excuse to turn to him in the night and wind her arms around his neck and kiss him back. She would store up memories instead, and squirrel them away to comfort her in the bleak future that stretched ahead when her job here was over.

Stella's absence meant that Finn took the opportunity to go back to work, and with Alex at school, and the days brightening, Kate decided to spring-clean the house again. She was being paid to be a housekeeper, she reminded herself, so she might as well keep house.

She started at the top, blitzing the bathroom and all the bedrooms. Inspired, she pulled out the beds, vacuumed into the corners, dusted and polished and tidied away the clutter that irritated Finn so much.

When it came to his room, Kate was quite embarrassed at the state she had reduced it to. Each side of the bed reflected their different personalities. On her side, the table could hardly be seen beneath a mass of moisturisers, tissues, pens, nail polishes, emery-boards, books, magazines, bits of jewellery and cotton wool, buttons, torn price tags, receipts...ah, there was that comb! She had been looking for it for ages.

Good God, where had all this stuff *come* from? It was as if her things were breeding and taking over Finn's room. They had yet to make a break for his side of the bed, but it could only be a matter of time.

Kate swept everything away and gave the table a good dust before heading round to Finn's side. Tidying *his* table wasn't going to take long. Apart from the businesslike lamp and electronic alarm clock, all that marred its pristine state was a small pile of coins that he had emptied out of his pocket last night.

Hardly a mess, then, but Kate was determined to tidy them away as a point of principle. Unsure what to do with them, she opened the little drawer under the table and was about to tip the coins in when she stopped. A framed photograph was lying face down in the drawer.

Slowly, Kate lifted it out, knowing what she would see when she turned it over. Isabel.

Of course Finn would have had a photograph of her by his bed, where she would be the first thing he saw when he woke, and the last before he slept. Kate's heart cracked at the thought of how much he still loved and missed his wife.

Holding the photograph in her hands, she sank down onto the edge of the bed. He must have put it away when they had first discussed sharing a room, unable to bear the thought of seeing Isabel's face when another woman was where she ought to be. The contrast would have been too much to take.

Kate looked down at Finn's wife. She had been so beautiful with those great, dark eyes and that sweet smile. How could Finn ever think about putting anyone in her place?

Biting her lip, she leant forward to slip the frame back into the drawer and saw a letter on the floor. She must have pulled it out inadvertently when she took out the photograph. She picked it up, not wanting to read it, but unable to avoid a glimpse of the words 'love always and for ever' written in Finn's black, decisive scrawl.

Always and for ever.

Kate stood up, put the letter back underneath the picture and closed the drawer.

Time to get real. Finn was never going to love her the way she loved him. It was no use hoping and pretending and burying her head in the sand. Oh, of course she had told herself that she knew that Finn still loved Isabel, but she hadn't really *believed* it until now. Finn didn't say things he didn't mean. He *would* always love Isabel. He would love her for ever.

Kate was quiet that evening, but when Finn asked her what the matter was she smiled and shook her head. 'Nothing. I'm a bit tired that's all.'

And when they went to bed, she clung to him, unable to imagine how she was going to be able to bear saying goodbye, but knowing that she was going to have to find a way.

Stella came back from what she called her 'tour of England' three days later, and immediately noticed the change in Kate. 'What's wrong?' she demanded bluntly the moment the two of them were alone. 'Have you two had a fight?'

'Of course not,' said Kate.

'I know Finn can be difficult,' said Stella, clearly not believing a word, 'but you're so good for him, and Alex is so happy now, too,' she went on. 'I couldn't bear it if it didn't work out between you and Finn.'

Stella was just going to have to bear it, the way she was, Kate thought sadly.

'Really, Stella, everything's fine,' she lied.

They all went to the airport to see Stella off. Kate was sorry to see her go, and not just because her departure meant that there was no excuse to stay with Finn and Alex any longer. Finn's sister could be abrasive at times, but her heart was in the right place, and Kate liked her warmth and her enthusiasm and her no-nonsense approach.

Even so, she was surprised at how emotional Stella got when it came to say goodbye. She hugged Kate tightly and thanked her for everything she had done, and then she turned to her brother.

'You keep hold of Kate,' she told him as she kissed him. 'She's just what you need.'

Alex was the last to be hugged. 'Make sure your father doesn't do anything stupid,' said Stella.

'Promise you'll let me know as soon as you've decided a date for the wedding,' were her parting words before she went through passport control.

'I don't know how I'm going to tell her that there's not going to be any wedding,' sighed Finn as they headed back to the car with that sinking sense of anticlimax that comes with a goodbye. 'She's never going to forgive me.'

'Maybe you won't have to tell her,' said Alex, scuffing along beside him.

'What do you mean?'

'You could go ahead and get married.'

Finn stopped in mid-stride. 'Alex, the only reason Kate and I have gone through all this is because you said you didn't want a step-mother.'

'I wouldn't mind Kate,' said Alex.

There was a moment of appalled silence while the three of them stood as if marooned in the middle of the busy terminal. Kate didn't dare look at Finn, but she could feel the tension in him. She was going to have to do something to defuse the situation before he exploded.

'I think you'd soon get bored of me,' she told Alex in an effort to pass it off lightly. She even managed a feeble smile.

Alex's mouth set in a stubborn line. 'No, I wouldn't.'

'I'd be very strict. It would be bed at eight o'clock every night, and no television during the week. You wouldn't like that, would you?'

'No,' Alex admitted, 'but it would be better than you going.'

'All right, Alex, that's enough,' said Finn in a curt voice. 'Kate's done us a favour, but she's got her own life to live now.'

'But—'

'I don't want to hear any more about it,' he said with an air of finality and strode out through the doors towards the car park leaving Alex and Kate to trail silently behind him.

It was a tense drive home. Finn shut himself in his study as soon as they got back, telling Kate that he was going to do some work and didn't want to be disturbed. Alex sulked in her bedroom with Derek.

Kate wasn't sure what to do. Carry on as normal, she supposed. Whatever normal was now.

At least she could spare Finn an awkward conversation, she decided, and quietly moved all her things out of his room and back into her own before he had to ask her to do it. She made up her old bed and changed Finn's sheets. Now they could pretend that nothing had ever happened.

Finn didn't notice until later that night when he had said goodnight to a still sullen Alex. He came downstairs to find Kate wiping down the cooker and trying not to think about what she was going to do next.

'You've moved your things,' he said abruptly.

'Yes, I...I thought it would be easier that way.'

'Easier?' Finn repeated as if he didn't understand the word.

'We agreed that we would only sleep together until Stella left,' Kate made herself say.

'I know we did, but—' Finn stopped, thinking better of what he had been about to say. 'Yes, you're right of course,' he said stiffly instead. 'There's no reason to carry on now that she's gone.'

'No,' she said bleakly.

There was an uncomfortable silence while the air between them churned with things left unsaid.

'It was just a temporary thing,' said Kate to reassure him that she understood and wasn't going to make a fuss.

'Yes.'

Another agonising pause.

Kate wrung out the cloth she had been using to wipe the hob and fixed on a bright smile. 'I'd better think about what I'm going to do next,' she said, setting about the draining board. Anything other than look at Finn and having to resist the impulse to throw herself into his arms and beg him to let her stay.

'Do you know what you want to do?'

Stay with you and Alex. 'No,' said Kate instead, 'but I'm sure I'll find something. I can always go back to temping.'

Finn took a turn about the kitchen. 'I don't suppose you would consider staying on, would you?' he asked suddenly, as if the words had been forced out of him against his will.

Kate's heart lurched into her throat and she had to swallow hard before she could speak. 'I thought you were going to try and manage without a housekeeper?'

'That was the idea—it was what Alex wanted—but it's going to be difficult. Rosa's definitely not coming back and...well, the truth is that I've been thinking about what Stella said,' he went on in a rush. 'Alex does need a woman here and she likes you. She's just been begging me to ask you to stay.'

He stopped. 'Would you think about it?'

Kate twisted the cloth between her hands. She wanted to stay, but would she be able to bear just being a housekeeper now?

'I don't know,' she said hesitantly. 'I don't think I could be a housekeeper for ever.'

'I was thinking more about you being a wife,' said Finn.

Kate's head jerked up to stare at him incredulously. 'A *wife*?'

'I don't seem to be putting this very well.' Finn raked a hand through his hair with a sigh. 'I'm trying to ask if you'll marry me.'

Kate opened her mouth and then closed it again. 'But... *Why*?' she managed at last.

'It seems sensible,' he said. 'It would solve the problem of finding someone to look after that dog for a start!'

'Oh, well, that seems like a good enough reason!'

'Seriously,' he said, 'Alex likes you. She's never been prepared to even consider the idea of having a stepmother before, but you... you're different. I think she'd be happy if you were here as a housekeeper, but she'd feel much more secure knowing that you would always be there for her.'

Kate looked at him, her brown eyes very clear. 'How would *you* feel?'

'I'd be happy, too,' said Finn, meeting her gaze. 'We've got on well these last few weeks, haven't we?'

Kate thought about the long, sweet nights, about waking to his lips on her shoulder, about being able to turn in the dark and run her hands over his lean, hard body. 'Yes,' she agreed huskily. 'Yes, we have.'

'It would mean you wouldn't have to go back to temping. Of course you could get a job if that's what you wanted to do, but you've always said that you're not that interested in a career, and you're much better at making a home than at being a secretary.'

Finn seemed determined to outline all the advantages for her, as if she couldn't work them out for herself. 'It might not be very romantic,' he told Kate, 'but there are worse reasons for getting married than comfort and security.'

True, thought Kate, but she had always imagined getting married for the best reasons. She had managed to crumple the dishcloth into a tight ball, and she bit her lip as she went back to wiping around the sink.

'What about Isabel?' she asked.

Finn hesitated. 'I think she would understand. She would want what was best for Alex, and that's what I want too.'

So he wasn't even going to pretend that he was marrying her for love, thought Kate, mindlessly wiping. Perhaps it was better that way. She wouldn't have believed him if he'd tried to convince her that he wanted her for more than practical reasons.

It was funny, she thought wistfully. You could dream and dream about something but somehow when it came true it was never quite as you had imagined it.

Be careful what you wish for, she reminded herself with a wry inward smile, or you just might get it. Only a few minutes ago, she had longed for Finn to ask her to marry him, and now he had. What was the point now in wishing that she could have his heart as well? She had known all along that it would always belong to Isabel.

Folding the cloth, she laid it carefully on the draining board. 'Can I think about it?' she asked Finn, amazed at her own calm.

'Of course.' Finn was a bit disconcerted by her self-possession as well. Not surprising, given how eagerly she had always responded to him. He must have thought that she would jump at the chance, Kate thought. 'I don't want to push you into something you don't feel comfortable with,' he said.

Kate looked at him. The only thing that would make her comfortable right then would be for him to put his arms around her, and tell her that he wanted her to stay, not for his daughter, not for his dog, but for him.

But you could only have so many dreams come true in a day, couldn't you?

She smiled at him a little remotely. 'I think I'll go to bed,' she said. 'It's been a long day.'

Finn watched her as she went to the door. 'Kate,' he said abruptly, and she turned.

'Yes?'

'I...' Whatever it was, he changed his mind. 'Nothing,' he said.

'*Marry* him?' Bella stared across the table at Kate. The three of them were sitting in their favourite bar where Kate had called them to an urgent case conference the following evening. 'You're not seriously considering it, are you, Kate? *Are* you?' she added suspiciously before slumping back in her chair and shaking her head. 'You are!'

'Well, I've been thinking about it,' said Kate with a shade of defiance. All night and all day, in fact. She hadn't been able to think about anything else since Finn's proposal.

'I know it's not the kind of marriage we all dream about, but we can't all have the perfect romance like Phoebe. I bet I wouldn't be the first woman to compromise on the starry-eyed stuff,' she said defensively. 'There might be other things that would make up for all that.'

'Like what?'

'Respect…liking…giving a little girl love and security…'

'You wouldn't be marrying Alex—or the dog, before you drag him into it,' Phoebe pointed out astringently. 'Of course marriage is about compromise, but not about something so important and especially not for a born romantic like you. I think you'd need to know that Finn loved you to be happy.'

'You've changed your tune, haven't you?' said Kate, cross with her friends for filling her mind with doubts again just when she thought she had made up her mind. 'You were the one trying to set me up with Finn in the first place.'

'We thought you'd be good together, and you would, but not unless Finn really is over Isabel. Of course he won't forget her, but he needs to move on. He needs to want you for yourself, not just as a glorified housekeeper.'

Phoebe leant forward seriously. 'You can't go through life believing that you'll always be second-best as far as he's concerned.'

It would be better than going through life without him, thought Kate. She had lain awake long into the night, missing Finn beside her and envisaging the days and weeks and months and *years* ahead when he wouldn't be there. If she married him, she would at least have him physically. They might have children, and that would bring them closer. She might never have what Isabel had, but she would have *something*. That would be better than nothing, surely?

'You deserve the best, Kate,' said Phoebe. 'Second-best isn't good enough for you.'

'I think it might be,' said Kate.

Phoebe and Bella did their best to caution her against making a terrible mistake, but the more Kate thought about it, the more marrying Finn seemed the right decision. Their marriage might not be perfect, but at least this way she would be able to see him and touch him. Alex would be there, too. They could be a family.

And what, after all, was her alternative? Bella might say that she would meet someone else, but Kate didn't want anyone else. She only wanted Finn. The thought of life without him, with nothing to do except miss him, was too awful to contemplate.

Finn was waiting up for her when she got home. 'I've been thinking about what you said last night,' Kate said baldly as she watched him fill the kettle and set it to boil for tea.

He turned, grey eyes suddenly alert. 'About marrying me?'

'Yes.'

'And?'

'And...' Kate opened her mouth to tell him that she would marry him when she suddenly realised that she couldn't do it, and she stopped. She couldn't live with him and not tell him that she loved him. It had been hard enough up to now. Could she really spend years not being completely honest about how she felt?

'I was going to say yes,' she told him honestly, 'but I've just realised that it wouldn't be fair on either of us.' Slowly she drew the ring he had bought her off her finger and laid it on the table.

'I thought I could go with all the sensible reasons,' she said. 'I told myself that they were good enough reasons to get married without love, but I think now that they won't be. We nearly made a terrible mistake, Finn,' she said, meeting his eyes squarely. 'I think it's better if I go.'

Finn looked bleaker than Kate had ever seen him, but he didn't try to persuade her. 'Alex will be disappointed,' was all he said.

Alex was more than disappointed. Devastated would have been a better description of her reaction when Kate told her that she was leaving. 'But you said you would stay for ever!' she wailed. 'You promised!'

Finn's face was drawn. 'She had to say that while Stella was here, but you knew the situation all along. You knew Kate was just pretending.'

'She shouldn't have said it if she didn't mean it!' Alex burst into tears, and rushed out of the room.

Kate was close to tears herself by that stage. 'Shall I go after her and try and explain?'

'No, leave her,' said Finn wearily. 'She'll come round.' He pinched the bridge of his nose between his finger and thumb. 'I just hope she doesn't make the new housekeeper's life hell. She's more than capable of it.'

In fact, when the agency sent along a new girl a couple of days later, Alex went out of her way to be nice to her, and punished Kate by ignoring her completely. Megan was an

Australian on a working holiday. She was friendly and competent, with a very pretty, open face. Kate tried to be pleased that she was going to fit in so well, but her heart cracked with misery and jealousy as she packed her case.

Finn had said that he would drive her back to Tooting. He asked Alex if she wanted to come, but she shook her head in an offhand way and said that she would rather stay with Megan. At the last minute, though, she rushed out to the car as Kate was about to get in and threw her arms around Kate's waist to hug her tightly.

'Goodbye,' she said in a cracked little voice, and then, without looking at Kate directly, she ran inside again.

Kate's throat was so tight that she could hardly speak, and the tears rolled down her cheeks as she got into the car. She wiped them away with the back of her hand.

'She will miss you, you know,' said Finn apologetically. 'She's just upset.'

'I know. I'll miss her too.'

'Perhaps you could come and see us some-time,' he suggested. 'You could check that we're looking after that dog properly.'

At the moment the prospect felt as if it would be too much to bear. 'Perhaps,' she said.

It was all Kate could do not to howl as they drove away from the house. She felt as if a great weight was crushing her. Why, why, why had she chosen to leave? She should have stayed and then there would be no nice, pretty, friendly Megan for Finn to go home to, to get to know, to make part of his life.

Heartsick, Kate let Finn drive her back to her old life. He carried her case into the house from the car, and upstairs to her bedroom, while Kate lingered reluctantly in the hall. She had always liked this house, but with Bella out it felt cold and lonely. Like her life was going to be from now on.

She was dreading the moment when she would have to say goodbye to Finn, but trying to keep her composure was such agony that she almost wished he would go. 'Thank you,' she said as he came down the stairs. Her voice was hard and tight, the only way she could speak without crying.

Finn seemed very close to her in the narrow hallway. Kate edged towards the front door.

'I should go,' he said, but he didn't move. For once he seemed at a loss to know what to do next.

'Yes,' said Kate. 'Alex will be waiting for you.'

He squeezed past her to turn to her on the doorstep. Kate gazed at him hungrily, as if storing up the memory of his stern face, and that mouth…she might never see him again, she thought in panic.

'Thank you for everything, Kate,' Finn said stiffly, and as if on an impulse leant forward to kiss her on the cheek.

It was only the briefest of touches, the mere grazing of cheeks, but Kate closed her eyes with longing. Instinctively, her hands lifted to his chest to cling to his shirt. 'Goodbye,' she whispered as she kissed his cheek in return.

They looked at each other for a long, desperate moment, and then her hands fell. Finn turned without another word and walked along the pavement to his car. He opened the door and, with one last look back at Kate, he got in and drove away, leaving her desolate and alone in the doorway.

One thing about misery, it made for a great diet. The weight fell off Kate as she struggled through the next few days, but she was too unhappy to appreciate the way her clothes had started to hang off her. She had signed on with an agency, but there were no jobs as yet, which was a pity. Money wasn't a problem after the generous cheque Finn had given her, but not working left her with too much time to think.

Too much time to remember.

Too much time to ache with longing for Finn and the life she had thrown away.

'You've done the right thing,' Bella tried to reassure her. 'I know it's hard, but it's better for Finn to deal with his feelings for Isabel first. He needs closure on that.'

'Closure? What does that mean?'

'It means he has to decide himself that it's time to accept her death and move on. Once he's done that, he can think about his feelings for you.'

'I don't think he has any,' said Kate drearily.

'In that case, it's just as well you didn't marry him, isn't it?'

Kate knew that Bella was right. All the reasons why marrying Finn would have been a bad idea circled endlessly in her brain, but none of them stopped her wishing that she was back in the house in Wimbledon, with Finn coming back from work, wrenching at his tie as he came into the kitchen. Alex would be sitting at the table doing her homework, and Derek would have picked the most inconvenient spot to lie as usual, so that she tripped over him whenever she moved.

The image of them all was so vivid, and her need to be there so acute that Kate pillowed her head in her arms and wept all over again. At the other end of the table, the cat stared contemptuously at her. It had already learnt to distrust the sound of crying which usually meant that the humans would be too preoccupied to think about feeding him.

Kate hadn't thought that it was possible to cry this much. She kept waiting to run out of tears, but after five days there was still no sign of them drying up. Her eyes were permanently red and puffy, and whenever she caught sight of her reflection she recoiled at how awful she looked. No wonder no one would give her a job! What was the point of being thin like this if the rest of you looked so frightful?

Bella put an arm around Kate's shoulders. 'Oh, Kate…' she sighed. 'What are we going to do with you?'

'I don't know,' wept Kate. 'I don't know what to do with myself either!'

'I've asked Phoebe to come round,' said Bella. 'You know how good she is in a crisis. Ah! That'll be her now,' she added as the doorbell went. 'I'll go and let her in. She's bound to be able to sort you out.'

Kate didn't even bother to lift her head. She loved Phoebe dearly, but there was nothing her friend could do about her raw, sore heart. Only Finn could make that better.

'Kate?'

That wasn't Phoebe. Kate stilled, her head still buried in her arms and her hair spilling out over the table where the cat toyed with a few strands in a bored way. It had sounded like Finn's voice. She must be imagining things.

'Kate!' A definite note of exasperation had crept into the voice, the faintly irritable edge that could only belong to Finn.

Very, very slowly Kate lifted her head. Finn was standing there, watching her with hard, anxious grey eyes. She stared at him, hardly able to believe that he was real, that he was *there*.

It was definitely him. Nobody else had that austere face or that mouth that made her melt just thinking about what it could do to her. But he didn't look quite the way he had done whenever she had fantasised about seeing him again. In her imagination, the sight of her had started a smile in his eyes which would slowly illuminate his face as he held out his arms to her.

This was real life, not a fantasy. She could tell by the fact that he wasn't smiling and his expression was one of puzzled irritation.

'Didn't you hear me?' Not *my darling*, or *I can't live without you.*

'Yes, but I didn't think it could be you,' said Kate obscurely.

The faint frown between his brows deepened. 'Are you all right?'

Kate knuckled the tears away from under her eyes. Why did he have to turn up now, when she was looking at her worst? The spurt of resentment was invigorating. After all her dreaming and longing to see him again, he was finally here refusing to follow the script!

'Do I look all right?' she asked tartly.

'You look terrible.'

'Sorry, but I've never mastered the art of blubbing gracefully.' Kate sniffed and blew her nose on a tissue.

It was strange. Part of her was really quite cross with Finn for catching her unawares and being so obtuse about the state she was in, but the rest of her was unashamedly joyful just to see him again. It was as if all her senses had suddenly woken up from a leaden sleep and started carrying on like cheerleaders, high-kicking and shaking pompoms about with sheer exhilaration.

Finn pulled out the chair beside her and sat down. 'What are you crying about?'

'What do you think?' asked Kate almost rudely.

'Is it Seb?'

'*Seb*?' It was so long since she'd given Seb a second thought that it took Kate a moment to work out who he was talking about. 'No, of course not.' She scrubbed a tissue under her eyes. 'Why would I be crying about Seb?'

'You told me that you loved him once,' said Finn. 'I thought that maybe when you said that you couldn't marry me without love you were thinking about him. I was afraid you might be hoping to get back together with him, and that it hadn't worked out.'

It was so far from the truth that Kate made a hiccupping sound between a sob and a laugh. She shook her head. 'No, I wasn't crying about Seb.'

'Then why?'

Kate didn't answer. 'What are you doing here, Finn?' she asked instead.

'I wanted to see you,' he said simply.

Blowing her nose again, she drew a jagged breath. 'Don't tell me Megan hasn't worked out. She seemed so suitable.'

'She's fine, but she's a bit bored with us,' said Finn. 'I think she would like to move on to somewhere more exciting.'

'She's bored with you?' echoed Kate, finding it hard to imagine.

'None of us is much company at the moment,' he told her. 'We're all miserable.' He paused. 'We all miss you.'

Kate stopped in the middle of wiping the tell-tale evidence of tears from her cheeks. 'You do?'

'Alex cries herself to sleep at night, the dog is pining, and as for me...' Finn shook his head. 'I miss you more than either of them,' he said.

Kate's heart began to thud. 'Really?' she asked huskily.

'Really.' He turned in his chair to face her. 'Do you remember when Stella left, she told Alex to make sure that I didn't do anything stupid? Well, I did something stupid. I didn't tell you how I really felt about you.'

'Why not?' said Kate, hardly daring to breathe.

'I was afraid you would think that I was too old and intense for you. You always seemed like so much fun. I couldn't believe that you would really be interested in someone like me. I kept remembering what you'd told me about Seb, and even if you hadn't wanted him again, it was obvious that a younger man like that—or that financial analyst of yours!—was going to be much more your type.

'I couldn't bear the thought of you leaving, though, so I tried to persuade you to stay by making it seem more like a job. And that really was stupid, as my dear sister explained to me at length,' he finished acidly.

'Stella knows about us not really being engaged?'

'She does now. Alex rang her and told her that I had been stupid just as she had warned. The next thing I knew I had my sister on the phone, demanding the full story and wanting to know why I had thrown away my best chance of happiness in years. I said that I had asked you to marry me and that you had refused, but it didn't take her long to prise the whole truth out of me. She couldn't believe what a mess I'd made of it. ''For an intelligent man,'' she said, ''you sure are stupid!'''

Kate gave a watery smile. She could practically hear Stella saying it.

'She told me that I should come back and tell you everything I'd left out before,' Finn said. 'So here I am.'

He looked down at his hands, and then straight into Kate's eyes, which were still red and swollen with tears, but shining now with hope. 'Can I tell you now, or would it make you uncomfortable?'

Kate swallowed the lump in her throat. 'No, I'd like to hear it.'

'I didn't tell you how much I love you,' he said. 'I didn't tell you how empty the house would feel without you. How empty my *life* would be without you.'

Taking her hands in both of his own, he held them tightly. 'I can manage the school run. I can walk the dog, and sort out the cooking and the cleaning. I can manage all of that, but I can't manage without you. And I want to do more than just manage. I want to be able to wake up and find you beside me. I want to come home and find you there.' He paused. 'I didn't tell you how much I need you, Kate,' he said in a low voice.

The cat chose this moment to yawn widely and stand up, presenting its bottom to their faces, and then sitting with a glare of affront when it failed to provoke the usual reaction.

There was a glow starting deep inside Kate, spreading out to every pore. Her fingers were curling around his. 'What about Isabel?' she asked as she had asked before.

'I loved Isabel,' he said quietly. 'Nothing can change that, but I don't feel as if part of my life is missing any more. I never expected to fall in love again,' he told Kate. 'I thought I'd had my chance at love, and that I'd never get another chance at that kind of happiness, and then you came along and turned my life upside down. You made me happy again.'

His fingers tightened around hers. 'You're not a replacement for Isabel,' he said. 'I never wanted anyone to be that. You're *you*, and it's you I need.'

The grey eyes were warm and serious as they looked into Kate's. 'If I had said all that to you when I asked you to marry me, would your answer have been different?'

'Yes,' said Kate.

'So if I asked you again now…?'

Her eyes shimmered with tears. 'I'll say yes,' she promised.

Then there was no more talking and Finn had pulled her into his lap and was kissing her so hungrily that Kate thought that she would pass out with happiness.

They might have stayed like that for hours if not interrupted by the cat, who was tired of being ignored and took a swipe at Finn's arm.

Jerking it back, Finn inspected the scratch. 'What did he do that for?'

'He's just looking for attention,' said Kate consolingly. 'He didn't mean to hurt you.'

'Well, he'll have to learn that I've got more important things to attend to at the moment,' said Finn, gathering Kate back into his arms, only to pause as a thought occurred to him. 'I hope he's not coming with you?' he asked in a voice of foreboding.

'I'm afraid so,' said Kate. 'I can't ask Bella to look after him. He won't be any trouble.'

Finn looked down at the scratch on his arm. 'I suppose the house is going to be taken over entirely by waifs and strays now,' he pretended to grumble, but he was smiling as he kissed his way along her jaw.

'Will you mind?' she asked, winding her arms around his neck.

'Not if you're there.'

Kate turned her head to meet his lips for a long sweet kiss. 'At least Stella will be happy now,' she sighed happily when they broke apart at last and she rested her head on his shoulder.

'Oh, no, she won't! You wait,' said Finn. 'We'll just get the wedding over, and she'll be nagging us about Alex needing a brother or sister.'

Kate laughed and kissed him again. 'I don't mind seeing what we can do about that,' she said.

'Anything to shut my sister up?'

'Anything,' said Kate.

MILLS & BOON® PUBLISH EIGHT LARGE PRINT TITLES A MONTH. THESE ARE THE EIGHT TITLES FOR NOVEMBER 2003

❧

THE FRENCHMAN'S LOVE-CHILD
Lynne Graham

ONE NIGHT WITH THE SHEIKH
Penny Jordan

THE BORGHESE BRIDE
Sandra Marton

THE ALPHA MALE
Madeleine Ker

MANHATTAN MERGER
Rebecca Winters

CONTRACT BRIDE
Susan Fox

THE BLIND-DATE PROPOSAL
Jessica Hart

WITH THIS BABY...
Caroline Anderson

MILLS & BOON®

Live the emotion

1003 Rom LP

MILLS & BOON® PUBLISH EIGHT LARGE PRINT TITLES A MONTH. THESE ARE THE EIGHT TITLES FOR DECEMBER 2003

---❦---

AT THE SPANIARD'S PLEASURE
Jacqueline Baird

SINFUL TRUTHS
Anne Mather

HIS FORBIDDEN BRIDE
Sara Craven

BRIDE BY BLACKMAIL
Carole Mortimer

RUNAWAY WIFE
Margaret Way

THE TUSCAN TYCOON'S WIFE
Lucy Gordon

THE BILLIONAIRE BID
Leigh Michaels

A PARISIAN PROPOSITION
Barbara Hannay

MILLS & BOON®

Live the emotion

1103 Rom LP